It was a good five meters long. It had six legs, the front pair shorter and more articulated than the others, ending in a fierce-looking set of claws. A brown and gray carapace that looked like, and was probably as hard as, stone protected its body. As Jackson watched, it suddenly roared, the sound echoing through the water around him, and threw itself against the bars of the cage.

"What," he asked simply, "am I supposed to do with that?"

"Your task is to subdue the u!xan, and bind its front legs with the coil I have given you."

"Subdue that?" Jackson held up the rope. "With this?"

"Its mandibles have been removed—it cannot harm you, if you are quick enough, and strong enough."

He shook his head. It still looked more than capable of harming him.

"The test will begin when the cage door opens. It will end when you have successfully bound the u!xan, or . . ." she paused, "you can no longer continue."

Books in the Dr. Bones series:

THE SECRET OF THE LONA
THE COSMIC BOMBER
GARUKAN BLOOD
DRAGONS OF KOMAKO
NIGHTMARE WORLD
JOURNEY TO RILLA

DR. BONES™
Book 5

Nightmare World

By David Stern

A BYRON PREISS VISUAL PUBLICATIONS, INC.
BOOK

iBooks
Habent Sua Fata Libelli

iBooks
Manhanset House
Dering Harbor, New York 11965
bricktower@aol.com • www.ibooksinc.com

Library of Congress Cataloging-in-Publication Data
Stern, David. Nightmare World.
        (Dr. Bones) "A Byron Preiss Visual Publications Book."
p. cm.
        [1. Fiction—Science Fiction—Hard Science Fiction. 2. Fiction—
Science Fiction—Crime & Mystery. 3. Fiction—Science Fiction—Alien
Contact.] I. Hagen, Joel. ill. II. Title. III. Series: Dr. Bones.

ISBN 978-1-59687-946-1
January 2021

Thanks to Jill, Bones and Howard for the help,
Paul Preuss for the texts,
and David and Byron for the chance . . .

Table of Contents

Prologue.. 1

Chapter One..7

Chapter Two...17

Chapter Three..33

Chapter Four..45

Chapter Five... 61

Chapter Six... 77

Chapter Seven...89

Chapter Eight.. 105

Chapter Nine...125

Chapter Ten.. 139

Chapter Eleven.. 151

Chapter Twelve..167

Chapter Thirteen....................................... 185

Chapter Fourteen....................................... 197

Epilogue... 213

Appendix: Notes on !Xaka! Society..................... 219

Technical Data Bank......................................221

Prologue

The stars returned as the great plastic spaceship *Keshir* emerged from the fold in space she had used to cross the galaxy.

Inside one of the ship's passenger cabins, the old shri known variously as Reelys (to companions from his'er days in the Legion of Ares) and Ahnast Jhiilla (the name s/he had used as a member of the Galactic Council) retracted an eyestalk and instructed the *Keshir* to block the spectacular view outside. The ship complied, opaquing the cabin walls, but not before Reelys caught a glimpse of the molecule-thin solar sail unfurling behind the ship that would propel the *Keshir* on the rest of her journey.

The stars were replaced by the previously interrupted information displays Reelys had been examining. A secondary panel flashed, notifying Reelys that the *Keshir* had been passed for transit. Normally, the ship would have been detained upon her emergence from the black hole event horizon, her cargo and personnel carefully checked by those shri manning the transfer station. But the *Keshir*'s arrival had been anticipated, and station personnel had foregone the normal procedures in the interests of speed.

Satisfied, Reelys directed one of his'er eyestalks to the main display screen and resumed his'er studies.

To humans, shri most resembled giant jellyfish, thanks largely to the array of tentacles that hung from the balloonlike central body. But the hermaphoditic shri were high-altitude, rather than aquatic, dwellers. They floated on air, held up by their buoyant central gas bag. And shri were several orders of magnitude smarter. In fact, in this, the year 2465 by human reckoning, they were the tacitly acknowledged rulers of all intelligent species in the galaxy, maintaining loose but effective control over the United Worlds through an intimidating bureaucracy that would have been the envy of Imperial Byzantium.

Once in a great while, though, they ran into a problem that bureaucracy was not equipped to handle. This was one such problem.

As did most of the shri's problems of late (at least, it seemed that way to Reelys), this one involved the !xaka!—an expansionary, aggressive race whose constant squabbling had more than once threatened to disrupt the relative stability of the United Worlds.

The latest incident, the one that had brought about the conference the *Keshir* was now journeying toward, was the destruction of a luxury cruise liner, and the death of the five hundred innocent passengers aboard. One of the !xaka! clans, the G!at, had mistaken the pleasure yacht for a rival clan's troop transport, and obliterated it with one of their own planetcracker ships.

Idly flexing his'er massive gripping tentacles, Reelys (the name s/he preferred to use now that s/he was no longer a member of the council) wondered if the shri had made a mistake in not confining the !xaka! to their home world of Ahng after first defeating them in battle. Perhaps that would prove to be the best solution in this instance—it would certainly be the easiest way to avoid further trouble.

S/he and the twenty other shri aboard the *Keshir* would find out when they reached Sersic-4—another week's journey ahead.

The secondary panel lit up suddenly in a series of brilliant flashes, announcing an incoming communication. Reelys touched a small pad on the panel once, then twice, and the main display cleared. The image of another shri appeared.

"*Keshir.*" The shri on the screen did not speak, but rather used the different light-emitting organs with his'er brain to send a series of flashes. Except when among humans and !xaka!, who used spoken language, this was how shri communicated.

This shri—Soshera—coincidentally a member of Reelys's extended family—was now speaking directly with all twenty-odd shri aboard the *Keshir*. Soshera had arrived at the G!at mining colony on Sersic-4 prior to the main shri negotiating party. Reelys noted the discoloring splotches on the mantle that shrouded his'er body, an inattention to form that indicated stress—no doubt due to the talks currently taking place.

"*I am glad you all have come. The situation here has worsened. The !xaka! have begun to threaten each other with violence. Several thinly disguised troop-carriers were turned back at the transfer station.*"

"Primitives." This from one of the other shri aboard the *Keshir*. "*We will not permit them to carry their clan wars out into the greater galaxy.*"

"*Indeed. One wonders how they managed to survive themselves and reach space at all,*" another put in. Reelys indicated his'er agreement. !Xaka! society was rigidly structured, and fiercely competitive; the most powerful clans monopolized certain products and/or services, and maintained armies of slaves to protect their interests, both political and economic. Three times in the past hundred years, the !xaka! had gone to war among themselves in dispute over those interests.

The *Keshir* and those aboard her were here now to prevent a fourth such war from breaking out.

"What is the current situation?" Reelys asked.

"The clan representatives are awaiting further instructions from Ahng—as we have been awaiting your arrival. None have shown the slightest interest in any of our compromise proposals."

"Incredible."

"Incredible indeed, Ahnast. And you have yet to meet the clan delegates in person."

"That is an honor I shall try and delay as long as possible. I will see you shortly."

"I will look forward to it. Soshera out."

The other shri aboard gave their farewells, and the screen went blank again.

In some respects, Reelys, after years of associating with humans, !xaka!, hlidjski and numerous other races, now preferred to communicate in spoken language. Though visual communication was much faster (the entire conversation with Soshera had lasted less than five seconds), more nuances of expression, more shades of emotion could be detected when communicating verbally. Still, in this case, there was no missing the underlying tone of the conversation.

Soshera was warning Reelys and his'er fellow travelers aboard the *Keshir* that they faced a truly momentous task.

The crisis in this instance concerned black holes—more specifically, the creation and placement of black hole transfer stations. These stations were the key to practical interstellar travel, and the shri maintained exclusive control over the technology involved. Not just for the economic benefits, as humans and !xaka! often complained (though the duties imposed through the transit stations were not inconsiderable), but for very practical concerns as well. The forces involved in the creation of a black hole were primal, potentially incredibly destructive. Giving a race as essentially unpredictable as humans or !xaka! access to those forces would be like handing a fusion bomb to one of the lower order of cloud-dwellers on the shri home world of Griynsh.

Certain protocols in the treaties establishing the United Worlds now called for the shri to build one such station in the outlying spiral arm of the galaxy. This suited those !xaka! belonging to the clan G!at, who maintained control of all !xaka! mining operations, because that was precisely where the highest concentration of the heavier elements would be found. But most of the other !xaka! clans (for their own selfish reasons) now wanted the next station built nearer the !xaka! home world of Ahng. Only one station could be built, only one sector of space thus exploited: Billions of credits rested on the choice of location.

It was no wonder the !xaka! were ready to go to war over it.

But the last such war had spread to their colony worlds, and disrupted interstellar traffic for several years. Thus, the shri had demanded this special conference.

Reelys found the entire affair upsetting to his'er notions of how intelligent beings should conduct themselves. Compromise and recognition of their mutual

concerns was in the best interests of all the clans—
another war would, among other things, only result in
delaying the construction of *any* transfer station. S/he did
not, however, necessarily expect that particular argument
to appeal to any of the !xaka!.

Consternation unconsciously reflected in a subtle
change of hues in his'er mantle, Reelys requested the
Keshir to access further information on !xaka! history and
customs.

Chapter One

"History lies."

Dr. Ezekiel Bones, hands tanned almost as dark as the old wooden lectern they rested on, voice pitched just loud enough to be audible in the amphitheaterlike lecture hall, smiled at the puzzled reaction those words caused in his new students. A hundred of them were crammed into the room—kneeling in the aisles, leaning against walls, even sitting on top of desks in the back rows. He'd warned the department chairperson to expect a larger-than-usual enrollment for this class, and tried to get her to free up one of the larger auditoriums for it. But she was new, and not entirely convinced that Zeke's reputation would be enough to pack in more than the usual twenty or so students for an Introductory Archaeology class.

He slid his hand over a small colored panel fastened to the side of the lectern—it chirped softly, waiting instructions. "Send a record of the class attendance to Dr. Langston's terminal," Zeke said quietly. The panel chirped again, acknowledging his request.

For the next session of this class, he hoped to have that larger auditorium.

Behind Zeke was a huge display screen: If he'd wanted, his words could be scrolling down that huge screen now, as he spoke, and his students could be downloading his lecture directly to their own computers. But the screen was blank. In this, as in so many other instances, he preferred to do things the old-fashioned way.

He leaned forward on his elbows and broadened his smile.

"I say again, history lies,"—and now he was speaking to one member of his class in particular, a serious-looking young man with close-cropped blond hair, who wore an old-fashioned three-piece suit and sat in the front row, listening intently.

He looks out of place here, Zeke thought. An actual student.

Zeke stepped back from the old wooden lectern—another thing that seemed out of place here, among all the metal and plastic. He'd found it in a storeroom overflowing with things from Old Yale, before they'd moved the university underground, and immediately rescued it, liking the palpable connection it gave him to Yale's grand tradition.

He began to pace the stage, continuing his talk.

"History tells us of empires that ruled the Earth—and then vanished overnight, without a trace. Of conquering generals, who led their vastly outnumbered armies to miraculous victory after miraculous victory—only to die in a curtained-off bedroom, betrayed by a woman's kiss. Of hordes of barbarians that decimated country after country, bent only on the complete and utter destruction of civilization."

In back of the serious-looking young man, two other students, a boy and a girl, had stopped staring at each other, and were now staring at Zeke. They were dressed in casual, loose-fitting, loudly patterned prints—much more typical student clothing. New Yale had a policy of adjusting the temperature in its underground campus to mimic the passing seasons outside, and students generally adjusted their wardrobes to match, even though most of them wouldn't dream of leaving the climate-controlled domes of New Haven City till the scorching summer heat broke in a few months. A group of three or four young men in the back row who looked like football players and had been talking loud enough to be calling signals also fell silent.

Obviously, none of them were expecting Introductory Archaeology to be like this, especially on the first day of classes. Most had probably been drawn here out of curiosity—the chance to see Dr. Ezekiel Bones himself—rather than genuine interest in the subject. Intro had a reputation as an easy course; last year's professor had rarely strayed far from the standard texts. Those students who, clued in by veterans of that course, had come to this class anticipating something similar, didn't know what to make of this lecture—or of Dr. Ezekiel Bones himself, for that matter. In his one-piece black coverall, Zeke—his sandy-colored hair bleached almost blond by the fierce African sun, his lanky, six-foot body hardened by exercise—probably looked as out of place as anything in the room.

That was all right with Zeke. He knew that before you could teach your students anything, you had to get their attention. So if making outrageous statements about history helped him do that, well . . . that was fine, as was looking different from the classic archaeology professor.

"History, in short, is full of lies. Of course," Zeke continued, now shifting his gaze across the auditorium, drawing in the rest of the class, "I'm not telling you anything new. You've all been admitted to this bastion of higher learning because you're at least normally intelligent"—a few snickers at that around the lecture hall—"so you probably know that. Many of the so-called classics—Herodotus, More, Selabi—contain passage after passage of outright lies."

The serious-looking young man in the front row frowned, and raised his hand.

Zeke smiled, and held up his own hand to forestall the question.

"I know what you're going to say—and you're right. I am exaggerating. The authors of those books had no intent to deceive. But when a historian of three thousand years ago told the truth, it was the truth as seen by someone who believed the Earth sat at the center of a universe ruled by a not-so-benign group of gods. Even when we look at history written in relatively recent times, we have to take into account that everything we see is being distorted by the historian's particular world-view. The global expansion of the European countries in the second millenium A.D. was treated by their historians as the spread of civilization—but to the native populations of the New World, it was genocide. And yet virtually all the histories written about those native populations was written by the Europeans as they swept across the Americas. What are we to make of their stories of the Incas, or the Iroquois?"

The room was silent, but then, Zeke had meant the question to be rhetorical. He had his students' attention.

"Those stories are necessarily subjective—one person's account of what happened, ordered by that person's conscious and unconscious biases. Some of them—Diaz's *Conquest of Mexico* comes to mind—serve as a good introduction to those otherwise vanished cultures. All too often, those stories will be the only thing some people ever learn about them. But there's a lot more to a culture's history than the written records left behind by it or its conquerors—and you lucky people are here to learn about all those other things." He paused, and smiled again. "This is Introductory Archaeology. If you've wandered into the wrong class, now's your last chance to leave."

Nobody moved.

Zeke supposed he had their attention.

"Good. Well then—this semester I'll be teaching you all about the science of archaeology—its methods, its goals, even a little bit of its history. To start, I'd like to consider how the kind of written records I've talked about actually do serve the archaeologist, and to do that, I'd like to go back in time a few hundred years, to the late nineteenth century. . . ."

And Zeke began to talk about Heinrich Schliemann, whose belief that Homer's epic poems were not just tales spun around some long-ago campfire, but in fact were stories (however distorted by time) of real places and real people, had resulted in the discovery of Troy, and a long-forgotten Mycenaean culture.

One of the students—the young woman in the second row whom he'd noticed before—raised her hand tentatively. Zeke nodded.

"Professor, could I just ask a quick question—before you go on with the lecture and all. This list of classes you passed out"—she held up a sheet of printout—"well, these aren't the same topics Professor Langston covered last year, and—"

"That's right."

"So you'll be using a different set of holoprojections, then. Maybe Professor Chang's from two years ago, or—"

"No, I don't intend to use any holoprojections. I'll be here, every class, in person."

They young woman slumped back in her seat. Zeke smiled broadly. He'd just come from a month and a half of relaxation on his family's African estate. During those six weeks, he'd tracked a pride of lions across the Serengeti, constructed and programmed his most ambitious artificial intelligence system to date, and even begun a rigorous program of martial arts training under Jackson Charles' careful guidance (*aikido*, his friend called it). He certainly didn't intend to let a computer simulation do his teaching.

He continued his lecture.

"Schliemann's success inspired many others to follow in his footsteps. One of them felt that, as Schliemann's study of the Homeric epics had led to the discovery of Troy, the Greek legends of King Minos might lead to the discovery of a similar civilization. His name was Sir Arthur Evans.

"Evans is a particular hero of mine. His discovery and careful reconstruction of the palace at Knossos on Crete is a model for all archaeologists—as is his exhaustive study of his findings. But Evans's excitement over the discovery of the Knossos palace led him to make a tragic mistake—the kind of historian's mistake I was talking about earlier. I don't want to bog you down in the specifics—not yet, anyway"—nervous laughter swept the room—" but I do want to give you the general outlines of the problem. From his digs at Knossos, Evans recovered hundreds of shards of pottery inscribed with rudimentary symbols. He found these symbols consisted of two different alphabets."

Zeke half-turned to the screen behind him.

"Herb, show us the alphabets."

The huge screen suddenly came to life, displaying two sets of symbols, clear black images against a white screen.

"On the left, you see the signs used in Linear A—on the right, those used in Linear B."

"A lot of those are the same," the girl in the second row blurted out. She looked around, then slumped back quickly in her chair, suddenly embarrassed at speaking out.

Zeke nodded. "That's right—they do use a lot of the same signs, though Linear B, the later script, is more complex. Evans believed B was simply a refinement by the Minoans, to enable them to more clearly distinguish between certain sounds. But he was wrong.

"To understand why, you have to understand the magnitude of Evans's discovery. He had found a civilization that traded with the Pharaohs of Egypt and ruled the seas of the Mediterranean a thousand years before the flowering of Greek civilization—a civilization that, according to the physical evidence he'd unearthed, perished at the height of its glory in a volcano as powerful as a dozen fusion bombs. It's a wonderful story—the kind of history Herodotus would have written—but it's not true.

"A young Englishman named Michael Ventris, using something called frequency analysis, was able to decipher the tablets, and prove Linear B was in fact a simple variation on Mycenaean Greek—using the Linear A symbols instead of the traditional Greek alphabet. This meant the Minoan civilization, far from being at its height during the time the Linear B script was used, had in fact been dominated by the Mycenaean Greeks.

"Frequency analysis is a linguist's tool, but we archaeologists aren't shy about borrowing from other sciences—in this class, we'll use a bit of physics, a bit of anthropology, and I suspect we'll even find a use for some history from time to time."

"Will we get to use your spaceship for field research?"

The question came from one of the football players in the back of the auditorium. His friends all laughed.

Zeke laughed too. He had just decided who would be doing the class's first methodology project.

"I don't think so—I don't plan on using the *Ostrom* for a long time. She's halfway across the galaxy right now—"

He stopped short.

Against the back wall, the classroom door swung open. Zeke's first reaction was one of surprise—monitor robots patrolled the corridor outside, preventing entrance while classes were in session within. Only an emergency or an override command could get you past those robots, and he had heard no alarm. So it had to be an override command, but who—

A figure stepped through the doorway. Marty Szigmond—Zeke's closest friend. He was still wearing the blue and yellow coverall from the *Ostrom*'s cryogenic chamber.

The look on his face told Zeke something had gone very wrong.

"Class dismissed," Zeke said, starting up the steps toward his friend.

"They took her before we knew what was happening, Zeke. We couldn't do a damn thing."

They were in Zeke's office. Marty sat on Zeke's desk, his feet dangling a good half foot off the floor, chewing on something he'd found in the office refrigerator. Zeke stood in the corner next to a large globe, tracing his finger back and forth across its surface, thinking. He gave the globe a sudden, angry spin.

"I knew this was a bad idea."

"Hell, I knew it was a bad idea too," Marty said. He hopped off the desk with a loud *thud*. Marty was hlidjski, Earth stock genetically engineered for life on a high-gee planet. He was short, square, and immensely powerful. He was also more than a little bit overweight.

"Sylvie knew it was a bad idea. Kadak!xa knew it was a bad idea. Only none of us knew it was gonna be a trap." He looked accusingly at Zeke, as if daring him to blame one of them for what had happened.

"All right," Zeke said, sighing heavily. "I didn't mean to suggest it was your fault." He pressed a finger against the spinning globe, stopping its rotation.

This was the time of the academic year Zeke liked best. It meant a fresh start for everyone. His bookcases were neatly organized, his desk spotless and immaculate, free of the clutter that he knew would accumulate over the course of the semester. Herb was in place and raring to go—the last of the bugs ironed out. And he'd made a good start with the students today, he knew that (at least until Marty had shown up). By the time he was through with them, they'd be beating down the doors to sign up for his Methodology class next semester. He'd even gotten a few ideas about that today—thinking about Evans again brought to mind a dig that had been going on off the shore of Crete. If he could work it out with Suzanne, that would be a. . . .

He shoved school, students, archaeology, and all related matters to the back of his mind, and faced Marty again.

"Tell me everything that happened—from the time you left Earth until the time you came back. And don't leave out a single detail. Kadak!xa's life may depend on it."

Marty nodded. "And Sylvie's, Doc. Don't forget about her. She's still there, you know."

"I know," Zeke said. "Now, start from the beginning. . . ."

Chapter Two

It had started simply enough—Zeke's ship, the *Ostrom*, had left Earth two weeks ago, after Kadak!xa had received an abrupt summons from her family on Ahng. "Our father is dying," it had said. "You must come at once."

Kadak!xa could not refuse. She hadn't seen her father in over a dozen years; after escaping slavery in the nitrate mines on Narokoran, she had joined the Legion of Ares as a mercenary, and then BEC, as a special assistant to Zeke Bones. She had not returned home to Ahng at all in the intervening time, partly out of fear of being recaptured by her G!at masters, partly because she had simply been too busy. But the thought of the one who had helped bring her into this world, who had raised both her and her brother Ho!xa, leaving it without her saying goodbye was intolerable. She had to go—and when she made it clear to all concerned that she would not be dissuaded, Zeke had insisted she borrow the *Ostrom* so she could reach Ahng as soon as possible.

In retrospect, that decision seemed like a very bad idea. To Marty, to Zeke—

—And especially to Sylvie Pharr, who sat in a small cave on the island of N'Gossa, shivering violently and cursing herself for a fool for ever making the trip.

She had been on Earth, visiting the Bones estate in Africa with Zeke and the *Ostrom*'s other crewmembers, when the message had come through from Kadak!xa's family. At the time, Sylvie had been happy to go. Not only was Kadak!xa a long-established acquaintance, but she'd actually thought there might be a story in the trip. The intergalactic rumor mills were working overtime; the word was a clan war could break out at any minute, and Sylvie, as one of the most recognized (and one of the best, if she said so herself) reporters United Communications Interplanetary had, wanted to be there.

Besides, after that fight with Zeke, Earth had suddenly seemed like a very small planet.

Sylvie didn't know why he'd decided it was too dangerous for her to visit Ahng; he knew risk was part of her job, and that she was willing to take chances to get a good story. She'd been with him on some of his expeditions when things had gotten a little rough, and she'd more than handled herself—he knew that. And wasn't it her articles about "Ezekiel Bones" (renegade son of the Bones family, ex-Academy of Mars, ex-Legion of Ares, current professor of archaeology at New Yale University, the man who'd forced the giant Bones Energy Corporation—BEC—to commit a large share of its fortune to funding a foundation for cultural treasures and convinced them to put an entire spaceship, the *Ostrom*, at his disposal for that purpose) that had made him famous across the galaxy?

It wasn't fair to ask her to stop taking those chances, no matter how genuine his motives. And she didn't want to think about his motives right now.

Sylvie shivered and cursed again.

Her cold-suit, which had been so warm when she'd put it on an hour ago, now seemed far too thin; she wished she'd let Marty send down those heating units from the *Ostrom*. But he and the ship were both long gone, and even though she had hundreds of different electronic gadgets hidden in her jumpsuit, none of them were going to protect her from the cold.

In the tunnel outside her cave, she heard the !xaka! workers scurrying back and forth with construction supplies as they struggled to repair a breach in the wall. There had been a minor earth tremor last night, and it had collapsed a section of the workers' complex she was staying in, exposing the structure to the sub-arctic weather outside.

She felt like she would freeze to death if they didn't fix it soon. Her hands were numb; she hid them under her armpits, trying to restore some feeling. She cursed the wind angrily, rocking back and forth hugging her knees tightly to her chest.

She should never have volunteered to stay behind. The rigid !xaka! caste structure paid little heed to such creatures as reporters, and her press credentials, which had opened so many doors for her in the past, had so far done very little for her here beyond get her down to the planet.

It was all very depressing.

She reached up with a folded edge of the cold-suit and brushed a teardrop out of the corner of her eye before it froze. Her eyes were tearing from the wind, she told herself. She was not crying. Sylvie Pharr did not cry.

Once, when she was five or six and had been forced to dress for a party she didn't want to go to, she'd thrown a fit—screaming, sobbing, the works. Her father stopped it cold in its tracks.

"Sylvie," he'd said, in that wonderful accent of his. "You must never cry like that again. You'll wash out all the colors in your eyes, and they'll turn white—just like a hlidjski's." She'd stopped right away, because she liked her eyes the color they were—a fierce jade green, just like his. She didn't want that to change. And by the time she'd gotten old enough to know that he'd been lying to her, the habit had sunk in. Sylvie hadn't cried very much at all when she was growing up.

The last time was when her parents were killed.

A rustling sound in the cave drew her attention.

"Sylvie?"

"Here, Ho!xa." She stood, her long black hair cascading down the back of the cold-suit, and quickly wiped away the rest of her tears.

It wouldn't do for the host to see her crying.

Ho!xa moved across the cave toward her—a half-shuffling, half-slithering motion, using all his legs to help slide his massive body across the floor. It looked clumsy—but Sylvie knew !xaka! could move like lightning when they had to.

As he approached, she involuntarily shuddered.

Since their first encounter, back in the late twenty-fourth century, numerous studies had been conducted on the dynamics of human-!xaka! relationships. All agreed on one thing: The two races found each other mutually repellent—to humans, !xaka! looked like big bugs (more specifically, Sylvie thought, giant earthworms), while humans resembled oversized versions of the sea parasites the !xaka! feared as the proverbial plague. Still, since Narokoran, Sylvie had come to know and even (in a strange sort of way) care for Kadak!xa.

But a whole planet full of them—

She felt frail, and vulnerable, even though the !xaka! in this complex were all Kadak!xa's family and friends, and thus, hers.

She hoped.

"Sylvie—food?"

Ho!xa held out a small, clear bowl in one of his first-segment hands. Steam rose out of the bowl and wafted toward the cave ceiling. For a moment, Sylvie just stood there staring, transfixed by the sight of food. She hadn't eaten since yesterday.

Then she took the bowl. It warmed her hands instantly. Nodding thankfully to Ho!xa, she raised it to her lips and swallowed.

It was terrible. It tasted like a tart pea soup—but at least it was hot.

She finished all of it.

"Thank you, Ho!xa," Sylvie said finally, approximating as best she could the various clicks and grunts of the !xaka! language.

Ho!xa indicated his acknowledgment. She held the bowl out for him to take, wishing there was more. She was still very hungry.

He clicked his mandibles together in agitation. "Sylvie—the bowl."

She looked at it closely.

"I don't understand," she said, shaking her head. Was she supposed to clean it?

Ho!xa clicked his mandibles again, and shook his own head from side to side.

Sylvie had no idea what he wanted. Maybe there was some strange !xaka! etiquette she'd failed to observe.

Suddenly, a light came into his hooded, compound eyes. He slowly raised one hand in front of his mouth and moved his mandibles, pretending he was chewing and swallowing something, chewing and swallowing something.

"Sylvie—eat the bowl," he said.

Sylvie looked at him again.

"You can't be serious?" She looked down at the thing in her hand. She couldn't "eat the bowl"—could she?

Ho!xa took the bowl from her and held it up to her face.

It did smell kind of interesting.

He broke off a piece, and placed it in her hand.

Sylvie shrugged. The old traveler's motto came to her. When in Rome. . . .

To her delight, it was delicious—chewy and spicy, like a jerky. And it was filling. Considering what superb natural chemists the !xaka! were, though—they could control the chemical reactions that took place inside the stomachs in each of their middle six segments, synthesizing different compounds almost at will—she shouldn't have been too surprised.

She smiled at Ho!xa, and took the bowl from him.

He nodded his head in what she assumed was agreement/ satisfaction. "Sylvie—the tunnel is secure."

He was right. The omnipresent howling wind was suddenly gone. Already, she could feel the cave getting warmer.

"Sylvie—comfortable now?" Ho!xa raised the first of his body segments off the ground, hovering near her.

She nodded. "I feel human again," she said.

Ho!xa looked at her for a moment. His body posture indicated confusion. Then she realized what she'd said, and started to laugh.

"Sylvie—tomorrow you visit the Keep, find Kadak!xa?"

"Tomorrow, I'll try again, yes." The Keep was the center of the vast G!at commercial empire—a complex of magnificent, gleaming structures, located in the center of N'Gossa Island. Sylvie had been there twice since her first arrival on-planet, and had yet to be admitted to any but the lowest levels of the city, normally reserved for slaves and maintenance workers. And of Kadak!xa . . . she'd yet to discover a trace of her friend since the G!at sprung their trap.

"Sylvie—you are like a sister to Kadak!xa. She is very lucky."

Before Sylvie could say anything else, Ho!xa turned and left, moving out into the main tunnel, on his way back to his own small cave, one of thousands of others in this complex. In the dim lighting of the cave, his clan badge (the three bright gold stones of the taga!xi, circumscribed by the claw and shovel of the G!at, their hereditary rulers), was barely visible.

He was Kadak!xa's brother—half again as small as she was, as !xaka! males were smaller than females. He was different from her in other ways as well—obediant where Kadak!xa was rebellious, quiet where she was explosive, deferential rather than questioning. But then, he was a slave. A male slave, no less. Doubly useless. He'd probably had his shortcomings drilled into him since the day he was born. How would you expect him to behave?

Sylvie shook her head. She'd been to cities on a hundred different worlds, and she'd never seen such deliberate, strictly enforced extremes of wealth and poverty as here. The way the G!at treated Ho!xa's clan—

She snapped her fingers. This could be the angle she'd been seeking for her article.

She reached carefully into one of her travel bags and, one by one, pulled out three small globes the size of softballs. Her holocams.

The data solids were nearly full, she noticed—she'd probably have to go over some of the material she'd filmed in Africa to start this piece. There were some good shots of Zeke and Mahsi there, and that old, comfortable house. She hated to lose them. Still, she was supposed to be a reporter, not a tourist. And it wasn't like she was never going back to that house . . . probably.

She laced on the belt webbing that controlled the holocams and ordered them off the ground. They rose gently and took up position five feet away, hovering like a trio of giant dragonflies.

Sylvie faced them, straightened her hair, and began speaking.

"Slavery is now a historical curiosity for humans. But here, on Ahng, it is a fact of life. And quite an unpleasant one."

She had spent the last week experiencing just how unpleasant—although she realized it could have been a lot worse. Ho!xa could have lived underwater, like the majority of the planet's population. . . .

And what about Kadak!xa? How uncomfortable a fact of life was slavery for her right now?

A number of awfully unpleasant possibilities began to come to mind.

There was a good chance Kadak!xa had simply been killed during her capture—it had been a violent enough incident. Or she could have been sent off-planet, to one of the G!at colony worlds, perhaps, or maybe even to one of the !xaka! penal colonies.

Maybe she wasn't in the right frame of mind to start this story after all. Sylvie snapped the holocams off.

They fluttered to the ground slowly, and came to rest in front of her. She stared directly ahead, her gaze seemingly fixed on the cavern wall.

Her thoughts, of course, were elsewhere.

It was a week ago, and they were just entering orbit around Ahng.

"*Congo*, you are cleared for docking at Shuttle Station A."

"Thanks, Station A. We'll see you shortly. *Congo* out."

The ship's computer automatically broke the connection, and Marty turned to face Sylvie.

"That's it. They don't suspect a thing."

"And why should they?" Kadak!xa boomed. Her eyes gleamed with satisfaction. "We have taken great pains to erase all traces of this ship's true identity. The G!at will never connect this ship to Ezekiel Bones, or BEC."

"Or to you," Sylvie said. "And that's what's important."

The three of them were in the *Ostrom*'s main lab (or perhaps she should say the *Congo*'s main lab, since they had gone to so much trouble to change the ship's registry), the largest room aboard ship and technically just as easy to control the *Ostrom* from as anywhere else.

They had renamed the ship in order that the G!at, nominally still Kadak!xa's owners, would never know one of their escaped slaves (probably their most prominent escaped slave, thanks to the featured role Sylvie had given Kadak!xa in some of her articles) had returned to their own backyard.

They planned to dock with the orbital station, shuttle down to the planet below, visit Kadak!xa's father, and return to Earth with the G!at none the wiser. At least, Marty and Kadak!xa planned to return to Earth. Sylvie planned to go wherever her investigation of the rumors she'd been hearing took her.

"I thank you both for coming with me,' Kadak!xa said.

"It's no problem," Sylvie said. "Besides, it might be a story."

"Yeah, forget it," Marty chimed in, standing. "There's not a lot for me to do when Zeke has a class, except figure out new ways to get into trouble."

"I hope you do not intend on getting in trouble on Ahng, Marty Szigmond," Kadak!xa said. "Trouble—or attention of any kind—is the last thing we want."

"He'll behave," Sylvie said, glaring. "Or I'll take the ship and leave him here."

A soft shudder traveled through the ship.

"Welcome to Ahng," the *Ostrom* announced. "We've just docked with the shuttle station."

The three of them left the main lab, returned to their rooms for their luggage, and rendezvoused again at the airlock. Sylvie led the way out of the ship, Kadak!xa following. Marty brought up the rear.

The corridors of the G!at station were wide and curving; directly opposite her, as she left the airlock, a panel flashed in the wide, sweeping strokes of universal pidgin.

"Shuttles to the planet are this way," she said, pointing off to her left.

"Hold on a second," Marty said. He slapped the *Ostrom*'s bulkhead in farewell. "Take care of yourself, *Congo*."

"You too, Marty."

Kadak!xa grunted. "Hlidjski. Always talking to machines."

Marty raised an eyebrow in annoyance. "They're a lot better conversationalists than certain nameless !xaka! I know."

He ordered the ship's airlock shut, and commanded it to open again to his voice only.

They set off down the corridor.

Large, circular door panels, each decorated in the gleaming symbols representing one of the major !xaka!

clans, were scattered at regular intervals along the interior wall of the station. As they approached one marked with the G!at symbol, it dilated open.

A group of heavily armored !xaka! spilled out into the corridor, blocking the way ahead.

Sylvie came to a halt, exchanging a quick, troubled glance with Kadak!xa. She decided to bluff it out.

"Is there a problem?" she asked slowly, addressing one of the !xaka!.

In response, it hiss/click!ed angrily, but did not move. *Looks like there is*, she added silently.

"Hey!" Marty demanded, walking forward past Sylvie and Kadak!xa. "What are you doing? Get out of the way."

One of the !xaka! suddenly reared back and slammed him effortlessly against the corridor wall. Marty slid slowly to the floor, and lay still.

There was definitely a problem.

Sylvie heard the sound of another panel dilating behind them, and turned. Their escape route back to the *Ostrom* was now blocked by another group of !xaka!.

"They are *U!xani*," Kadak!xa said, rearing up on her third segment, twisting in all directions. "G!at warriors."

There were a dozen of them in all. Even the smallest was a good half-meter larger than Kadak!xa, and though Sylvie had seen more than her share of !xaka! before, there was something different about these. They looked sleeker—the ring of muscle between each of their eight segments more developed, their glittering eyes somehow colder. Each of them held a curved blade in one hand. . . .

No. That wasn't it at all.

The shining blades had been grafted directly onto one of their second-segment legs. They'd deliberately mutilated themselves.

"What do they want?" Sylvie asked.

"That seems obvious," Kadak!xa said. "Me."

Sylvie barely had the chance to ask herself how the G!at had found out about their arrival before another !xaka!—much smaller, possibly even a male—stepped forward. This one's body was covered with glittering ornament, and she (he?) wore the clan badge of the G!at as well.

"You are the escaped slave Kadak!xa," it began. "You are to be taken to the Keep and—"

Kadak!xa hissed and turned back the way they'd come, intent on returning to the *Ostrom*, on keeping her freedom.

A half-dozen of the *U!xani* seized her, and she disappeared from sight.

"Kadak!xa!" Sylvie screamed.

Marty rose to his feet, groaning, and started toward the writhing pile of !xaka!.

Another of the *U!xani* moved in front of them, cutting off their view.

"This way," it said in universal pidgin, raising its surgically altered leg threateningly.

Marty growled.

Sylvie yanked him back with all her strength—from the look in the !xaka!'s eyes, it would just as soon kill him as argue.

They were taken to a small, windowless room and held for an hour. Their repeated requests for information were ignored. And when they were finally released, Kadak!xa was gone.

"To the planet below, in the custody of her rightful owners," the !xaka! who escorted them back to the *Ostrom*'s docking bay explained. Among the myriad pieces of jewelry and electronic gear that adorned her body, per !xaka! custom, she also wore the clan badge of the Ghi!reeli—one of the many !xaka! clans allied to the G!at, Sylvie knew from the preliminary research she'd done for her story.

"Your ship," the !xaka! nodded, indicating the airlock.

"Hold it, just hold it." Marty folded his arms and glared at their escort. "We want to talk to Kadak!xa." He had on his most intimidating look . . . but their escort was one of the largest !xaka! Sylvie had ever seen, fully three meters long; physically, Marty could no more intimidate her than he could the *Ostrom*.

"Kadak!xa is gone." The !xaka! reared back on her fourth segment, towering over them. "Here is your ship," she repeated.

"We're not leaving without talking to her," Marty growled.

The !xaka!'s gill fringes lifted and flared behind her, a vibrant blue-green. Her voice turned harsh and threatening. "The slave is in the custody of her owners, hlidjski. Her life is theirs to do with as they see fit—to end, if they so desire."

"Can we talk to the G!at, then?" Sylvie asked.

"Impossible. They are within the station's inner ring. *Access is prohibited to* such lower-caste personages as yourself."

"Lower-caste? Who're you calling lower-caste?" Marty demanded.

Sylvie laid a warning hand on his shoulder. "All right—can we at least speak with her family? Her father is very sick."

"You wish to communicate directly with a slave?"

"That's right."

"A strange request." The !xaka! considered it for a moment. "You would have to obtain a channel directly to the appropriate workers' complex. Such requests do not fall within my area of responsibility," she said finally. With that, she turned and disappeared down the station corridor.

Marty watched her go with undisguised contempt. "Half-worm, half-bureaucrat. That's the worst combination I can think of."

Sylvie managed a short laugh. "Somehow, I don't think she's the last one we're going to run across."

Sylvie was right. It had taken them an hour to find the !xaka! who was responsible for communicating with the G!at workers' complex, and another hour beyond that to establish contact with Kadak!xa's family. It cost them an arm and a leg as well.

But by the end of the conversation, they'd gotten their money's worth.

"Sylvie Pharr—Kadak!xa's father is dead. He died several months ago," Ho!xa told them, after introducing himself. "Did she not receive my message?"

Sylvie's eyes widened, and she felt the hair on the back of her neck stand on end.

"Wait a minute." Sylvie looked at Ho!xa, then Marty. "You sent a message telling Kadak!xa her father was *dead*?"

"Sylvie Pharr—that is correct."

"You sent a message saying he was dead—not one saying he was dying, and that she should return here as quickly as possible?"

Ho!xa made a soft hiss/clickling sound—a noise Sylvie was to learn later meant much the same as a human *harumph*. "Sylvie Pharr—of course not. It would be too dangerous for her to come to Ahng."

It suddenly became all too clear how the G!at had captured Kadak!xa so easily.

The whole thing had been a trap.

"They knew we were coming," Marty said. He slammed the side of the console in disgust and turned away. "They suckered us halfway across the galaxy with a phony message."

More to the point, they had prevented Ho!xa's own message from reaching them. That meant they had to be monitoring all communications to and from their slaves.

Including this one, she realized.

"Marty Szigmond, what do you mean?" Ho!xa asked. "What message?"

"Ho!xa, we have to go now," Sylvie said gently. "But I'll talk to you again soon."

She broke the connection.

"What did you do that for?" Marty asked.

She told him. "The last thing we want is the G!at listening in while we make plans. Come on," she said, standing. "I can tell Ho!xa what happened to his sister once I'm down on the planet."

"Once you're down on the planet? You think the G!at are just going to let you waltz right in and make yourself at home?"

Sylvie pulled out her press I.D. "Yes," she said. "I do."

Marty spent the next fifteen minutes trying futilely to argue her out of going, finally throwing up his hands in defeat.

"Go ahead—get yourself captured too. Zeke's gonna have my hide anyway."

"The G!at will be far less interested in me," she assured him.

Marty allowed that, but wonderred why they had gone to such great lengths to capture Kadak!xa.

Sylvie explained. It was the reason she had been feeling like the whole affair was her fault. It was the reason she *had* to stay behind and try to help Kadak!xa.

There were millions of slaves on Ahng—the institution was the foundation of !xaka! society. Let those millions see that escape was possible, that their destiny was not fixed, and the stones of that foundation would loosen. Show them that escape was not only possible, but profitable, as Sylvie's own stories of Kadak!xa had done, and the whole structure could come tumbling down.

Seen in that light, it was a wonder the G!at hadn't tried to recapture Kadak!xa sooner.

Marty took the *Ostrom*, and left for Earth.

She took her bags and wangled her way onto a planet-bound shuttle, using her press I.D., the threat of United Worlds involvement, and several thousand credits. Mainly several thousand credits. She'd then managed to recontact Ho!xa, who had been surprised to see her, and even more surprised to find out she wanted to stay with him, rather than in one of the Keep's luxurious hotels.

That had all happened four days ago.

Sylvie sighed deeply, suddenly drowsy. She arranged her bags into a makeshift mattress, and lay down. Already it was warm enough in the dimly lit cave for her to take off the BEC coverall, though she had to leave her jumpsuit on underneath; she had nothing else to sleep in. She wanted (needed, probably) a long, hot shower. But that would have to wait till Marty returned with the *Ostrom*—and Zeke.

Zeke. She rolled over and sighed, determined not to think about him right now. Well, things could be worse—at least she wasn't cold anymore.

And if she got hungry, she could always eat another bowl.

Chapter Three

Jackson Charles crouched low in the dry grass, waiting.

He had been waiting for hours.

Sweat trickled down the bridge of his nose, beaded at the tip. He ignored it, as he ignored the dryness in his throat, the hunger pangs in his stomach, the slight cramping of muscles in his lean, six-and-a-half-foot frame. He remained motionless, as much a part of the surrounding landscape as the insects that buzzed softly around him, or the birds that flew silently overhead. Anyone—or anything—could have passed within a few feet of him without noticing his presence. He'd even used one of Zeke's bioservos to mask his scent, rendering him invisible to even the most keenly aware predators.

It was dusk on the Serengeti plain, and Jackson Charles was hunting.

Hunting almost as the Bantu warriors who might have been his ancestors had done a thousand years ago—except that he would use no spear, no weapon. What he hunted this day, he did not intend to catch.

Above him, the stars were beginning to come out, brighter here than he was accustomed to seeing them on Earth. The constellations, too, were different than those Zeke Bones had identified for him in the night sky outside

New Haven City. He found a few he recognized—Ursa Major, the Great Bear, Gemini, the Twins, and there, Betelgeuse, the brightest star in Orion's belt.

Orion, the hunter. He hoped that was a good omen.

Jackson himself was much more of a fighter than a hunter. Physical combat had always been second nature to him—he'd made his living off it for years, first in the death-pits of his home world of Xi Pyxis 2, and now as a member of Zeke Bones's team. But all the combat skills in the world weren't necessarily going to help him in this task.

Off to his left, the grass rippled slightly.

He trained the servo that had replaced his left eye on the spot instantly, scanning into the infrared, searching—

There. A blur of heat, moving slowly through the grass. He zoomed in on the spot, and commanded the servo to switch to the visible spectrum. The great shaggy mane of a full-grown male lion came into view.

Here was the prey he had been seeking.

A week ago, Jackson had seen this lion cast out from the pride he had once ruled, supplanted by a younger, stronger male. There had been a fight between the two, and the older lion had been severely maimed, one of its eyes bloodied and rendered useless.

Since then, the old lion had been starving to death. Great folds of skin hung loosely from his body; his ribs clearly shone through. Even his once-lustrous mane was dirty and faded as he padded silently forward through the savannah.

Jackson waited until the lion was about seventy-five feet away from him, then rose up slowly from the grass, in plain sight of the beast's good eye.

The lion tensed, and growled deep within his throat. But he did not run. Somehow, he sensed he was in no danger from this man.

Jackson reached into his pack.

"Here you go," he said softly, and tossed the contents of the pack across the distance between them.

The lion jumped back suddenly as the steaks landed in front of him. For a minute Jackson thought the animal was going to bolt. Then curiosity got the better of him, and he slowly padded back to where the meat had landed. He sniffed at it curiously, then raised his head to stare at Jackson.

"It's food," Jackson reassured him. "Eat it."

The steaks, which he'd sealed in a specially insulated pack to prevent them from both spoiling and broadcasting their smell for miles around had been cut last night from a freshly killed gazelle. The old lion must be ravenous. He should be gobbling them down like candy.

Instead, he continued to sniff at them.

Jackson had left the Bones family estate at sunrise this morning, intent on finding the lion and bringing the steaks to him. He knew what it was like to lose an eye, as he himself had lost one fighting in the deathpits. Jackson could not replace the lion's missing eye, as Bart Charles, his adoptive father, had replaced the missing eye of the young Jackson Franks. But at least he could prevent the great beast from starving to death.

"Come on," Jackson urged. "Eat, you old fool."

As if he understood him, the lion looked up at Jackson and gave a low, throaty growl.

Then he crashed off into the grass, disappearing from sight.

Jackson cursed softly.

"I told you—he will not take your offerings."

Jackson spun suddenly at the sound of the voice.

"If you want to show him mercy, kill him now, before he grows too weak to defend himself from the other predators."

"Mahsi—don't *ever* sneak up on me like that. I might have hurt you!"

The old Bantu headman laughed. "You? Hurt me? Why?"

"I wouldn't do it because I wanted to—oh, never mind," Jackson said, shaking his head. He stared into the grass where the lion had vanished. "Why won't he eat?"

Mahsi shrugged. "He will eat only what he catches."

"But he can't catch a thing in his condition!" Jackson protested. "He'll die!"

"Then he dies," Mahsi said flatly. "That is the law of nature—and it is still the law here. Survival of the fittest. The old must make way for the new." He softened his words by reaching up and laying a hand on Jackson's shoulder.

The two had become close in the last few weeks; in a way, Jackson was duplicating Ezekiel Bones's own relationship with Mahsi, finding in him the father he had lost on Xi Pyxis 2, as Zeke had received from Mahsi the affection his own father had never given him.

Mahsi had been Leo Bones's personal pilot, and had run this estate for him, as he now ran it for Zeke. He looked strong enough to run it for another generation, though his hair had gone completely white and the lines around his eyes had become crevices.

"What are you doing out here?" Jackson asked him.

"Looking for you, naturally. A message came through this afternoon from Ezekiel."

"Trouble?"

Mahsi frowned, and nodded. "I am afraid so."

"Without a doubt, you have the most amazing capacity for food I have ever seen."

Marty smiled. "This is hard work," he said, keeping his eyes fixed on Zeke as he began to chew.

Zeke repressed the urge to ask Marty which task he was referring to—eating the pizza they'd ordered or studying the printout that lay strewn across Zeke's desk.

That desk had gotten messy a lot earlier in the semester than he'd expected. His new A-I unit, Herb, had printed out some five thousand pages of detail on !xaka! society—all the references to slavery he could find—and they'd spent the night studying it . . . with nothing to show for their efforts but a messy desk.

"I can't find anything useful in this," Zeke said, tossing aside another stack of printout. "What about the *Ostrom*'s files—anything in there?"

"Let's see," Marty said. He crossed the small office and stood in front of Zeke's comterminal. "What's 'the word' these days?"

"These days? Oh," Zeke paused a moment, realizing that Marty hadn't been back since he'd installed the new system. "The password is *Suzanne*."

Marty raised an eyebrow.

"Suzanne? What happened to Sylvie?"

"She went to Ahng with you, remember?"

"Right," Marty nodded. "Who's Suzanne?"

"None of your business," Zeke said, turning back to the printout. He didn't want to think about Sylvie—or what she was doing on Ahng—right now.

Marty shrugged. "Com-pu-ter." He said the word slowly, pronouncing each syllable distinctly. This terminal was ancient equipment; it had difficulty understanding the simplest of commands.

"What's the word?" the system croaked mechanically.

"The word is *Suzanne*," Marty said, again speaking clearly.

The computer paused a moment, accessing Zeke's customized programming. Then it kicked into overdrive. Scanning lenses on either side of the screen zeroed in on Marty, held his image for a second.

. . . The face of a thin, dark-haired man, with a bushy moustache and a slightly amused smile, appeared on the comscreen.

At the end of the last semester, the school's officials had finally granted Zeke permission to customize the computer system in his office. New Yale, in its typical, unimaginative, bureaucratic fashion, had given their computer a cold, efficient personality, and the face and voice of a research librarian. The visual component wasn't the big deal to Zeke—but any system he had to work with so much he preferred to be a little more "user friendly," or even just friendly.

Zeke had spent almost a month wondering what kind of personality he wanted to give to his system. That of a famous scientist? Alumnus? Archaeologist? His own?

Then one night, reading in bed, the perfect solution struck him. Actually, it struck him just after he'd finished his book—*Star Begotten*. He'd shut the cover, and found himself staring at a picture of the author—a man who, for all his celebrated anger with the world, had been, as Zeke liked to think of himself, a realistic utopian. A man who, though born half a millennium before, would have taken very little time to understand and assimilate the world of the twenty-fifth century. A man Zeke felt he could have spent hours talking with.

But he'd settle for the next best thing.

So he'd gathered together all the information, all the old pictures he could find, and had spent the better part of a week constructing the simalcrum that Marty now stared at.

"Herb, access the data banks on !xaka! customs and institutions on the *Ostrom*'s system. Quick as you can."

Herb nodded. The screen went dark.

Marty turned back to Zeke.

"I forgot to tell you—Sylvie and I worked out a code to sneak messages to us when she files her news reports."

"When she files her news reports?" Zeke asked. "What makes her think the G!at are going to give her access to an open channel?"

"She said Galactic Worlds protocol."

"She can't believe that. *You* can't believe that. The G!at have very little interest in Galactic Worlds protocol. If she tries to send some kind of unauthorized message. . . ." He shook his head in disbelief. "What does she think she's going to do there?"

"I have no idea," Marty said, raising his hands helplessly. Zeke had already yelled at him for letting Sylvie stay behind—as if he'd had any say in the matter. He didn't want to start that whole argument again.

"Excuse me," Herb prompted. "I have a call for you, Zeke."

"Put it through," Marty said quickly, grateful for the interruption.

Zeke glared, and nodded his okay.

On the comscreen, Herb disappeared, and a woman took his place. She had long blond hair and classically beautiful features. Her skin was tanned almost as dark as Zeke's.

"Suzanne," Zeke said. "I was just going to call you."

"Zeke." She smiled, revealing two rows of perfectly even, bright white teeth. "You were right about the enrollment figures. Guess I'll have to get you that larger classroom."

"I guess so," he said. "Listen, Suzanne—something's come up that I need to talk to you about—"

"We can meet in the faculty cafeteria. Five minutes," she said. "Or maybe you'd like to come up to my office?"

Marty made a small choking noise in his throat.

Suzanne caught sight of him behind Zeke's shoulder. "Who's that?"

"That's Marty Szigmond—he's part of what I need to talk to you about. Marty, Dr. Suzanne B. Langston."

Marty waved.

Zeke took a deep breath. "Suzanne—I may need to borrow those holoprojections of yours after all."

He explained the situation. Suzanne—Dr. Langston—didn't take it too well, especially when Zeke refused to say how long it might be before he could return. She started making noises about Zeke's professional irresponsibility, but by the time she'd signed off, Marty realized her anger was mostly personal.

"Seems like she knows you pretty well, Zeke."

"We worked together a lot," he said defensively. "She's the new department chair."

"Chair, huh?" Marty was about to make a tasteless joke, then thought better of it. No telling how well Zeke had gotten to know this Dr. Langston in the last two weeks—though if he'd had to bet money, he would have laid odds that it wasn't all *that* well.

Zeke and women . . . it was a real puzzle. Somehow, his friend's relationships just never blossomed. And he'd never been able to figure out the relationship between Zeke and Sylvie. Especially after that fight they'd had the night before the *Ostrom* left. He'd been embarrassed to be in earshot of that.

"Hate to bother you, Marty." It was Herb. "Here's the printout from the *Ostrom*."

"Thanks, Herb." Marty picked up a sheaf of paper about half an inch thick and carried it over to Zeke. "Looks like more gobbledygook to me."

"Gobbledygook is one of my strengths," Zeke said. He cleared a space on the desk and set down the new print-out, then sat down to study it. Marty sat next to him, and took another slice of pizza out of the box. He chewed thoughtfully, all the while staring intently at Herb's face on the comscreen. Something about that face was awfully familiar. . . .

"This is hopeless," Zeke said half an hour later. He tossed the printout aside. It slid off the desk and onto the floor, taking the empty pizza box with it. "The problem with all this material is that it's too general. We need an expert."

Marty's expression brightened. "Shouldn't there be one here—at the university?"

"There is," Zeke said. "You're looking at him. But I don't know much beyond what Herb's found—only what Kadak!xa has told me, which doesn't do me any good in this instance. The !xaka! are not very revealing when it comes to details of how their society runs. You know the Galactic Museum or Griynsh, where one building is dedicated to each of the United Worlds races? Well, the one set aside for the !xaka! is just about empty. They won't even let the shri make copies of their treasures to keep there."

"What are you saying—there aren't any experts?"

Zeke shrugged. "There have to be."

Marty snapped his fingers. "Hasn't BEC done business with the !xaka! before, on Ahng? What about one of the officers that did the negotiations there?"

"There were no negotiations—just straight cash transactions." Zeke rubbed his chin thoughtfully. "No, we need someone who's had to learn the nuts-and-bolts of !xaka! society in order to talk to them, like an ambassador, or a Galactic Worlds Councilor—"

He smiled, and turned to Marty.

Marty's expression changed then, as if he'd gotten faintly sick to his stomach.

"Now wait a minute," he said, wagging a finger. "There's got to be someone else . . .?"

"You know any other ex-Councilors?" Zeke asked.

Marty shook his head.

"All right, then," Zeke said, rising from his chair. "Herb—get me the shri ambassador."

It took Zeke a day to locate the ambassador and deliver his message. Reelys had it within a few hours after that.

It was a welcome interruption from the talks—the degree of hostility between the !xaka! clans had been surprising. Perhaps, in the years since retiring from the Galactic Council, his'er memories of being a Councilor had dimmed slightly, the ferocity of the arguments s/he had been involved in muted with time.

Or perhaps the Galactic Council had never been quite like this.

At any rate, news from old Legion companions was always welcome—especially news from Ezekiel Bones. But the news in this message was thoroughly upsetting.

First hand experience had taught him'er how important such abstract concepts as status and honor were to the !xaka!—but to go as far as they had to recapture an escaped slave. . . . It hardly seemed worth the effort. Surely the G!at had more important things to worry about.

Certainly their representatives here did. What little progress had been made in the talks on Sersic-4 had resulted in a loss of support for the G!at position among its allied clans. Several times in the last few days, the G!at representatives had stormed out of discussions, or renewed their threat of open warfare. The shri had convinced them to stay—so far. But the idea of remaining here until a consensus acceptable to all was reached . . . that was inconceivable, not only to the G!at but to all the !xaka! clans. They all seemed more concerned with using this forum as an excuse to air their disputes with one another than for solving the matter at hand.

Reelys also had begun to suspect that the clan representatives here were simply not authorized to settle the issue, that they had come more as a concession to the shri than to solve anything.

Hovering in front of the main panel in the cabin, s/he opened a communications channel to the base orbiting Sersic-4.

"*Soshera.*"

"*Ahnast. Our thoughts go with you. We will keep you informed of our progress here.*"

"*As I will keep you informed of what happens when I reach Ahng.*"

"*I wish you success. Soshera out.*"

"*Keshir out.*"

Reelys signed off and filed a course for the *Keshir* that would take the ship to the Nemesis black hole transfer point, and a rendezvous with Ezekiel Bones and the *Ostrom*.

The thought occurred to him'er that perhaps it was foolish to expect the !xaka! on Ahng to be easier to reason with than those here.

Perhaps it was foolish to expect !xaka! to be reasonable at all.

Chapter Four

The first time Sylvie had seen one of the !xaka! floatcars, she'd just laughed. It looked like a giant bathtub, with a clear plastic shell that closed over the top. It seemed incongruous that a race so physically imposing as the !xaka! used such an unimpressive vehicle as their primary method of transportation.

Now, though, as the one that would take her directly to the Keep rose gently off the ground, she concentrated less on the car's looks and more on holding down her lunch.

Riding a floatcar was worse than the wildest roller-coaster ride of her life. On her previous trips, traveling over the rocky landscape outside the workers' complex, the car had hugged the ground so tightly Sylvie she was sure they would crash any second. And inside the Keep, navigating the vast network of tunnels that honeycombed the ancient structure, they had taken turns so tightly and at such sharp angles that Sylvie had to hold on for dear life to prevent herself from smashing against the car's walls.

Today she'd brought her holocams, to get this wild ride on film.

She also needed them for another reason. Sylvie Pharr intended to do a little unauthorized exploring this morning.

The floatcar emerged at top speed from the underground tunnels of the workers' complex, and swung into the gleaming shadow of the Keep. Sylvie caught her breath. She'd seen this view of the G!at stronghold several times, and it had yet to pale for her. It was like moving from the crew lounge for a BEC construction ship to a high-society party aboard one of the space yachts.

Her first trip out to the workers' complex had been at night, during the !xaka! equivalent of rush hour, when the cars had all been crowded with workers returning home. She had been too preoccupied with Kadak!xa's capture and her own nervousness to catch more than a glimpse of the city behind her. Now, as it became visible, she wondered how she could have concentrated on anything else.

She decided this was also worth catching on film. Deftly manipulating the control webbing on her belt, she positioned her holocams to focus on as many different views of the city as possible. She quickly checked the images on her wrist monitor, making sure the holocams were all functioning, then settled back and concentrated on the view directly ahead.

The city sprawled out in all directions, as far as she could see. Towers of all different shapes and sizes dominated the skyline. Most were of gleaming metal and resembled nothing so much as giant fusion weapons rooted to the ground. A few slimmer ones, made of stone, looked like the ancient minarets of Cairo. The overall effect was stunning—it reminded her of photographs of Old New York, before the floods.

Oddly enough, the center of the city was the least built up—a single, squat structure, black hued, became visible for a moment before the floatcar curved around a bend and it disappeared, lost behind more of the gleaming towe s.

As they drew closer, the multilevel structure of the city became clearer. In many instances, older buildings served as the foundation for some of the larger towers—not too surprising, as this was one of the oldest cities on the planet. It had also served as the center of government for the last five centuries or so. More than any other, she supposed, this city, the G!at Keep, embodied !xaka! civilization; its physical stratification paralleled the stratification of the society itself. To find a slave in one of the towers would be as rare as finding one of the Councilors in the tunnels.

Sylvie had also been to the shri home world of Griynsh, whose cities embodied the characteristics of that ancient, wise race. The cities there seemed to float on the clouds, things of beauty to be marveled at, experienced, shared. In their own way, the towers of the Keep were as beautiful—but theirs was a beauty designed to instill not admiration, but awe. A terrible beauty, a thing to be feared, like some fierce, elemental power.

As the car reached the edge of the city itself, her view of the world outside disappeared.

Sylvie shut down her cameras, and prepared for a little skullduggery.

"You will have fifteen minutes with the slave—no longer. I shall return for you then."

The warrior who had escorted her left quickly, and the circular door panel irised shut behind her.

Sylvie couldn't blame her for being nervous. If her superiors found Sylvie in here, the guard would more than likely be sharing Kadak!xa's cell—or worse. It was a big risk—but she'd been more than adequately compensated for it, Sylvie felt. As had all the other !xaka! she'd had to bribe to arrange these next fifteen minutes.

Sylvie had spent her first visit to the Keep just looking around, familiarizing herself with the city. The second time in, she'd made inquiries, and found a bar that some of the G!at soldiers frequently visited. The third time, she'd gone there and started nosing around, asking questions, letting it be known that the answers would be worth money. She'd spent quite a bit before that night was over.

She returned to Ho!xa with the news that Kadak!xa was alive, and being held in the lowest-level dungeons within the Keep.

Her next trip in, she'd gotten the name of one of the soldiers guarding her. Another trip, and she'd made contact.

And now, this morning, she had paid a great deal of money for the privilege of a short conversation.

She turned away from the cell door, and turned her attention to Kadak!xa.

Years before, she had been covering the riots on Narokoran when she had found herself sharing a drink in a spaceport bar with a particularly talkative !xaka!. After many drinks, this !xaka! (a slave of the G!at mining corporation that ran Narokoran) had blurted out that she would do anything to escape her "soul-numbing servitude." The next day, Sylvie had hidden that slave aboard an Earth-bound freighter.

Now, stripped of the jewelry and armor Sylvie had become accustomed to seeing her in, Kadak!xa looked much the same as she had that night on Narokoran. She lay motionless on the cell floor, her head turned away from Sylvie.

"Kadak!xa?"

The great head lifted, and turned weakly toward her.

It was only then that Sylvie noticed the scars criss-crossing her body.

"My God." She crossed the cell in an instant, kneeling down by her side. "What did they do to you?"

"Nothing I did not do to them—several times over," Kadak!xa said weakly. "It is still somewhat . . . painful to move—excuse me if I do not rise."

For the second time in as many days, Sylvie felt tears rush to her eyes. She forced them back.

"Just relax." She touched her belt, and one of her holo-cams flitted forward, hovering over her shoulder.

"Sylvie Pharr—what are you doing?"

"I'm getting this on film. When the United Worlds sees what these bastards did—" her voice quavered.

"The United Worlds has seen these 'bastards' do far worse, and done nothing. Besides, there are those who would argue that G!at have every right to do with me as they will. I am an escaped slave."

Sylvie shook her head. "Once Zeke arrives, you're going to be out of here very quickly," she said firmly.

"I do not think so," Kadak!xa said, exhaling wearily. "Here, the G!at do as they please. No law binds them, no rules exist to prevent them from disposing of me however they see fit. They can kill me, keep me here for a hundred years, or assign me to some meaningless task, on some nameless world—"

"Don't give up before we even try, Kadak!xa," Sylvie said.

Kadak!xa laid her massive head down on the floor again. Sylvie squatted closer, trying to think of something reassuring to say that wouldn't sound empty.

"How is my father?" Kadak!xa asked abruptly. "The G!at refuse to bring me news of him."

Sylvie hesitated. She had been dreading this moment.
"He is much worse?"

"I don't know how to tell you this," she began. "He's
dead."

Kadak!xa was silent a moment.

"But that is so fast—surely—"

"I'm sorry, Kadak!xa. He was dead before we even got
here. That was the message Ho!xa sent. The G!at
changed it to lure you here."

Kadak!xa shook her head weakly, and even that simple
movement caused her obvious pain. "That cannot be
true—"

"It is," Sylvie said.

The cell door opened suddenly, and Sylvie got to her
feet.

"You must leave, now!" the guard hissed, clacking its
mandibles in agitation. "One of the G!at o!xer is conducting an inspection of the cells. She is coming this way."

Sylvie got to her feet. The o!xer, from what she'd
learned so far, formed the majority of the vast G!at
bureaucracy, and were somewhere between the warriors
and the upper-caste Councilors on the caste scale.

"Zeke's on his way, Kadak!xa," she said. "Don't worry."

Kadak!xa grunted in acknowledgement, and lowered
her head to the floor again.

"Hurry!" the guard hissed.

Sylvie nodded, and pressed a handful of credits into
the guard's first-segment hand.

"Make sure she gets double rations," she said, meeting
the guard's eye.

"I cannot—"

"Give her your own, then," Sylvie said firmly. "You'll be
well rewarded. There's a lot more where this came from."

The guard hesitated, clearly torn between the money and the risks she'd have to take to earn it. Then greed won out.

"Yes, anything, but hurry!" the guard said, literally pushing Sylvie out of the cell. The door irised shut behind her.

"The floatcar station is down this hall and to your right," the guard said.

Sylvie nodded, and set off briskly in that direction. Behind her, she heard the sounds of other !xaka! approaching—the o!xer the guard had referred to, no doubt.

She hadn't exactly gotten her money's worth out of that transaction—she'd been promised fifteen minutes, and gotten about five—but at least she'd found out that Kadak!xa truly was alive. You were never quite sure what you were buying when you depended on greed for your news, and until a few moments ago, she'd been as ready for a knife in the back as she had been for a visit with her friend.

She reached the end of the hail, and paused. To her right, she saw the floatcar station. To her left was an empty corridor.

Sylvie took a deep breath, and turned left.

In the week or so she'd been here, she'd received more than enough news to confirm the rumors she'd heard on Earth. A clan war was coming—sometime soon, no doubt. She'd picked up hints of it in her conversation with the G!at soldiers. It seemed the G!at were in the middle of a massive weapons buildup.

Now she hoped to find, and film, some hard evidence of that coming war. The dungeons were on the very lowest level of one of the G!at towers, but somewhere above her, if those soldiers had been right, were offices for the higher-caste G!at councilors. Maybe she could visit those higher levels . . . with a little help.

Sylvie reached into her carrysack, and pulled out a small, almost translucent bioservo the size and shape of an eye. She pressed the top of it, and the servo rose out of her hand and down the long corridor ahead of her. Within seconds it was invisible.

Stepping completely out of view of the main corridor, Sylvie switched on the holocam monitor on her wrist, and began to study the images coming in from the servo's miniaturized scanner.

First she saw only the corridor she was now in; feature-less, except for the circular door panels the scanner passed by, all of them shut. Then the images stopped moving—the corridor had ended. Using the controls on her belt, she panned the servo left and right. More corridor stretched out in either direction.

She ordered the servo to the left. It traveled another long stretch of corridor, as unremarkable as the first, and Sylvie was beginning to wonder just how many prisoners the G!at actually kept down here. Then suddenly the door panels ended, and the corridor curved around a bend and began to slope upward. A path to the upper levels, Sylvie realized—but her excitement faded when she saw the path blocked by a number of G!at soldiers.

She commanded the servo back to the branch in the corridor, and this time had it go to the right. Another series of door panels flashed by—one covered with a sequence of markings caught her eye for a second—and then the corridor began to slope upward again, and again the slope upward was guarded by soldiers.

No way was she going to be able to sneak past either group of soldiers. The hard evidence she sought would have to wait for another time.

She commanded the servo to return to her. As it flashed past the strangely marked door panel she stopped it, purely on impulse, and studied the image.

Sylvie could speak and understand many of the !xaka! languages, but when it came to reading them, she wasn't quite as knowledgable. Still, she could manage a rough translation of these markings.

Her servo, it seemed, had stumbled across the !xaka! equivalent of a service closet.

Hmmm. What sort of interesting things would be in there?

She decided to find out.

Sylvie took another servo identical to the first out of her carrysack, and set it to hover in the corridor behind her. She then ordered the first away from the service closet and toward the "T" in the corridor. Keeping a close eye on the images from both on her wrist monitor, Sylvie set off.

Reason kept telling her not to do this. Reason that spoke to her, strangely enough, in the voice of Zeke Bones. That voice told her that the information she had right now on the clan war was important, and had to be delivered to him. It also told her that if she got caught now, Zeke would never get that information.

She told Zeke—the voice—to be quiet, that she didn't have enough information for anyone to act on yet, much less to do a story. Zeke was about to say something else when Sylvie came to the "T" in the corridor. She turned to the right, checking her wrist monitor. The servo behind her showed the image of a group of !xaka! entering the corridor she'd just left. The G!at o!xer, conducting inspections. She watched as one of the cell doors irised open, and the o!xer, a large, ostentatiously armored female, stepped inside, followed by an attendant.

Two !xaka! remained in the hall, flanking the door opening.

There went her back door. Now she had no choice. She had to get into that service closet—to hide, if nothing else—or she was going to end up in one of those cells herself. She sent the first servo ahead of her down the corridor, and when the images came back, showing the guards on the pathway up to the next level chattering among themselves, she walked quickly and silently ahead to the service closet.

A small panel, about the size and shape of her fist, was set next to the door at waist level. Its exposed surface was a thin mesh of gleaming silver—some kind of audio key, she decided instantly. Play it a certain series of notes, more likely clicks in this instance, and the panel would open.

Sylvie didn't have time to try and guess those notes. Her only hope was that there was some kind of master series of tones that the o!xer and her attendants were using to open all the cells and conduct the inspection. She tiptoed as quietly as she could back in the direction from which she'd come. When she reached the intersection of the two corridors, she stood with her back pressed tightly against the wall, and listened.

The inspection was preceding rapidly behind her—the repeated hissings, announcing the opening and closing of each cell door, came every twenty seconds or so. And just before every other one of those hissings, she heard a short series of clicks.

Sylvie pulled off one of her earrings, and slapped it directly onto the wall next to her. It stayed there, held in place by a microadhesive. The earring, in fact, was a highly sensitive, unidirectional microphone. But was it powerful enough to hear that master tone from a hundred feet away, and reproduce it accurately?

She returned to the service closet, removed her other earring, and held it in front of the door panel. This one acted as a receiver for the other. Now she had both an audio and visual tap on the approaching inspection party.

Her wrist monitor showed her that it was the o!xer's attendant actually giving the sequence of tones to open each door—and as the party drew closer, that code, that sequence of clicks became clearer.

There were now four more door panels, two on either side of the corridor, that remained to be opened and inspected before the o!xer came to the bend in the corridor, and saw her.

She saw the attendant approach the first of those four doors, and pressed the earring close to the silver mesh of the door panel. The attendant gave the requisite series of clicks, and the cell door in front of the o!xer irised open.

The door to the service closet stayed shut.

The inspection party emerged from that one cell, and crossed the hall to the next. Using the controls on her belt, Sylvie turned up the gain on the microphone in her earring.

She had the sudden, uncomfortable realization that the master tone that opened the cells might not open the service closet at all.

Again, the attendant gave the requisite series of clicks. And again, the cell door opened—and the service closet didn't.

Sylvie cursed silently.

The party moved to the next cell, barely five meters away from the corridor intersection and the microphone, thirty from where Sylvie herself now crouched down next to the service closet door.

The service door didn't open the next time either.

Sylvie began praying that the inspection party would turn to their left when they reached the corridor intersection. But just in case they didn't, she reached into her carrysack and pulled out a handful of magnesium flares.

!Xaka!, she knew, were painfully sensitive to bright light. If she could blind them as they approached, she might be able to slip away in the confusion and make it to the floatcar station.

The o!xer's party approached the last cell. The attendant gave the necessary tones—and at the same second the cell door irised, the service closet opened as well.

Sylvie breathed a sigh of relief and stepped through the door.

And then she remembered the earring she'd left fastened to the wall.

Shoving her carrysack into the door panel so it couldn't completely close, she ran down the corridor, pulled the earring off the wall, and turned.

She heard the last cell door hiss shut, and the o!xer's party move out into the corridor again.

She ran the next ten meters faster than she'd ever run in her life. She reached the service closet, pushed her carrysack through ahead of her, and dove into the room.

The panel irised shut behind her, just as her wrist monitor showed the o!xer's party turning the corner and heading in her direction.

That was too close, she thought, waiting for her heart to stop pounding.

She picked herself up off the floor slowly, and took in her surroundings. The service closet was a long, thin room, lit by a series of lights coming from indicator panels on one of the walls. She had no idea what the lights meant.

But on the other wall . . . a half-dozen vertical tubes, long clear pipes with pulsing streams of light inside, stood behind a clear glass panel. Pressing her nose to the panel, she saw the tubes extended up and down as far as she could see. She knew what those tubes were. Communications cables. Pay dirt, for Sylvie Pharr.

Now, even if she couldn't actually get to the next higher level, she could at least find out what the G!at were saying to each other up there.

Carefully, she removed the glass panel in front of the tubes, and set it down on the floor next to her.

She reached into her carrysack again and pulled out a small, clear piece of plastic, about the size of a playing card, with a series of thin wires running off the edge of it. One edge of the plastic was coated with a thick, cushioning tape, which she carefully removed, revealing a razor-sharp edge. She crimped the loose ends of the wires together, and fastened a small plastic connector to that end. She then attached that wire to one of her holocams.

She picked out one of the communications cables at random, and, using the sharp edge of the plastic card like a knife, sliced through the cable's outer sheathing.

Working very carefully now, well aware that a slip-up would probably alert everyone in the tower to her presence and exact whereabouts, Sylvie inserted the card directly into the path of one of the light beams. Using the cushioned tape she'd removed before, she fastened the outside edge of the card to the cable sheathing.

Finally, she relaxed, and slowly let go of the card, making sure it was securely in place. The G!at transmissions would continue uninterrupted, feeding through the plastic card, which would record and send copies of the data pulses onto the audio channel in her holocams.

It would be interesting to see what the G!at were talking about.

Fifteen minutes passed without interruption, then a soft buzz announced that the datasolids were full. Sylvie carefully retracted the plastic card, and the edges of the sheathing closed together again—there was practically no evidence that any sort of cut had been made in the cable.

She put the glass panel back in place, and scanned the halls outside with her servos. The inspection party had moved on.

Sylvie summoned her servos back to her, exited the service closet, and returned to the floatcar station.

For all the care she'd taken, Sylvie's visits to the Keep had not gone entirely unnoticed.

The guard she had so carefully bribed to visit Kadak!xa had an unfortunate fondness for lithium kryptophosphate—a substance that had roughly the same effect on !xaka! as alcohol did on humans. In other words, it made them drunk, and more than a little loose lipped. The night following Sylvie's visit, this guard was in one of the lower-level bars with enough credits to buy a round of lithium kryptophosphate for all the !xaka! in the house. She was in the middle of explaining how she'd gotten all those credits, when she slipped and mentioned Sylvie Pharr's name. Ultimately, this did her no real harm, but it did draw the attention of another customer there, an u!xani who surreptitiously moved within earshot of the guard, and noted everything that was subsequently said about Sylvie Pharr, the famous human reporter.

Within a few hours, all that information had made its way into one of the gleaming towers Sylvie had admired from outside the city. And inside that tower, one partic- ular !xaka! began contemplating exactly how Sylvie's presence could be used to help further its own plans.

Chapter Five

Zeke rubbed the stubble on his face idly, wondering if he ought to shave now or wait until he woke again in fifty or so years.

He, Reelys, and Jackson were all assembled in the *Ostrom*'s sick bay for their final medical check.

Jackson had come aboard almost two weeks ago, rendezvousing with them in Earth orbit as they were transferring the "Herb" system aboard the *Ostrom*. Ten days later, at the Nemesis black hole station several A.U.'s beyond Pluto, Reelys had joined them. They all spent several hours in the main lab talking about what had happened to Kadak!xa, and what they could do about it. Zeke's instincts had been right: Reelys's expertise proved invaluable.

Now he was trying to explain the course of action they had just taken to Jackson, who lay flat on his back on a diagnostic couch. Reelys hovered over him, jetting back and forth while holding an array of sensory probes in his'er tendrils. A biomicro floated next to the shri, its monitor screen displaying the results of Jackson's tests for Reelys to study.

This set of last-minute checkups was designed to insure none of them had developed any medical conditions since their last voyage on the *Ostrom* that might affect them during deepsleep. Reelys, who had counted physician among his'er duties in the Legion of Ares, was supervising the completion of the diagnoses.

They seemed strictly a formality to Zeke: His two friends looked exactly the same as when he'd last seen them, though he couldn't swear Jackson hadn't put on a little more muscle in that time. Every inch of his dark ebony skin looked as solid as the alloy plate of the *Ostrom*'s walls. Reelys, on the other hand, looked as frail as Jackson was solid; being insubstantial enough to defy gravity had given the shri a reputation as delicate creatures among other species, but they were formidable opponents—as both humans and !xaka! had had occasion to discover.

"It's simple," Zeke said. "The G!at's claim is partially based on the service they paid Kadak!xa for—the *vir'kash*, as it is known. I have filed a rival claim on behalf of the BEC Archaeological Foundation—we've been paying Kadak!xa for the last five solar years. And our *vir'kash*," he smiled, "is much bigger than their *vir'kash*."

"I still don't get it," Jackson said. "They own her, right? Why do they have to listen to a claim from you—ouch!" He made a face at Reelys, who withdrew a small needle from the crook of Jackson's arm and floated away.

"No, Jackson," Reelys said. "Ezekiel has filed the claim with Ahng's Diet of Monopolistics, the planet's governing body. The Diet is composed of members from all !xaka! clans, not just the G!at. And under United Worlds reciprocity agreements, they must hear our claim." The shri bent an eyestalk forward, peering closely at the biomicro's display monitor. "You check out fine, Jackson. Ezekiel?"

Jackson slid down off the diagnostic couch as Zeke jumped up onto it and lay back.

"Still—what are the chances of the Diet ruling in our favor?" Jackson asked.

"I don't know," Zeke admitted. "But the case will not necessarily be decided solely on its own merits."

"Meaning what?"

"Meaning that politics on Ahng is like politics everywhere else, only—ouch!—more so."

"Politics is perhaps the best way to describe it, Jackson," Reelys agreed, withdrawing the probe. "The !xaka! empire is ruled by a constantly shifting alliance of clans, each of which maintains a monopoly on certain services or products, each of which is continually jockeying for more power, more money, more influence."

"Money makes their world go 'round too, huh? I know that song," Jackson said.

"More than just money, Jackson," Reelys said. "Honor. The G!at have played the primary role in their planet's affairs for almost all of !xaka! recorded history, exercising great influence over the actions of many clans. The source of that power has always lain not only in their material wealth, but in their honor—the respect they have gathered for their actions over time."

"Which could work in our favor," Zeke pointed out. "If we make this issue too much trouble for the G!at, maybe they'll be inclined to give up their claim to Kadak!xa."

"They are accustomed to having their way in matters such as this, Ezekiel," Reelys warned. "They will not take kindly to interference by off-worlders in their own affairs."

Zeke sighed. Unfortunately, Reelys was probably closer to the truth than he was. The shri had told them all of the talks on Sersic-4—from the sound of things, they'd be walking into the middle of a pressure cooker on Ahng.

"Sounds like it could get sticky," Jackson volunteered.

"What could get sticky?" Marty asked, strolling into the chamber, a half-empty can of concentrate in one hand. Reelys had already given him a clean bill of health, so he'd started on what he and Jackson liked to call the "antifreeze." During the time they'd be spending in deep-sleep, their metabolic rates would drop to practically zero: Anything in their bodies when they went into deepsleep would sit there like a lump for the duration of the trip. They had to give up all solid food and anything else that might be difficult to digest for the period immediately preceding deepsleep. All they could have was this specially designed liquid concentrate.

Marty was through a six-pack already.

"What could get sticky?" he repeated.

"Oh, nothing." Zeke raised his head off the couch and whispered loudly to Jackson. "We'll count on Marty's diplomatic expertise to prevent any violent confrontations."

"Now we're in trouble," Jackson teased. "Maybe we should forget about the trip after all."

"Too late," Marty said, in between swallows of the concentrate. "There's no real food left aboard."

Jackson glared at him. "You're kidding, right?"

"The Diet meets near the N'Gossa ruins," Reelys said pointedly. "Perhaps there is a second request you would like to file with them, Ezekiel."

"Perhaps there is," Zeke said, glad for a chance to change the subject. Beneath their levity, he knew they were all pretty concerned about their missing friends. Kadak!xa could have been executed by now, or sent halfway across the galaxy to one of the !xaka! colony worlds . . . and he didn't want to think about where Sylvie was.

And the subject that Reelys was talking about had been on his mind, ever since he'd decided to return to N'Gossa. "But I think the chance of seeing their famous Scrolls is pretty slim—especially for a human." The natural antagonism between the two races had even been codified: By treaty, no human was to own a copy of any !xaka!ian work of art, or relic.

"Still—it would be quite a coup if they said yes," Marty added.

"I have to plead ignorance," Jackson put in. "The Scrolls?"

"The Scrolls of N'Gossa—that's the name the press gave them. Actually, they're metal—zinc, specifically," Marty said. "But Zeke knows more about them than I do."

"Doc?" Jackson prompted.

Zeke sighed. Once a teacher. . . .

"The Scrolls of N'Gossa," he began, "are the most valuable archaeological treasure on Ahng. Uncovered a hundred years ago, among the drowned ruins of ancient N'Gossa, the Scrolls are the only written records surviving of the planet's first civilization—and no non-!xaka! has ever been permitted to personally examine them. . . ."

"They are beautiful—are they not?"

Sylvie jumped back from the display case, startled. Her holocams, which had been hovering above her, recording, shot quickly to either side to avoid a collision.

She straightened and turned to look at who had spoken.

She saw an immense !xaka!, one of the largest in terms of sheer bulk she'd yet encountered. Most of its weight, though, seemed to be fat, rather than the toned muscle she'd glimpsed on the U!xani. The !xaka! (female, she assumed from its size) was also high-status, by the color of the gill fringes on the back of its neck, though curiously free of the flashy ornaments so many other high-status !xaka! favored.

"You frightened me." She glanced over the !xaka!, looking for one of the guards she had bulldozed into letting her into this building.

"Apologies, Sylvie Pharr. I did not realize you were so absorbed in your examination." The !xaka! raised up on her third segment and bowed, giving Sylvie a better glimpse of the vibrant purple- and blue-colored gill fringes that lay flat along her back.

Make that very high status, she amended. Sylvie was surprised this !xaka! was even speaking with her.

"Apology accepted," Sylvie replied. She must have been more than a little preoccupied. !Xaka! were not generally noted for their stealth—and this room (almost this whole wing of the museum, as far as she could tell) was deserted.

Then she realized the !xaka! had called her by name.

"You have me at a disadvantage," Sylvie said. "You know who I am—though I don't know how—but I don't know who you are."

"I am !Jng!xl. As for how I know who you are . . ." !Jng!xl motioned with one of her arms, indicating Sylvie's holocams. "Well, there are very few humans on Ahng— and even fewer reporters."

Sylvie smiled. "I've been noticing that as well."

Two other !xaka! entered the room, wearing the same clan badge as !Jng!xl.

"My *o!xer*," she said. "Attendants."

Sylvie nodded. They bowed.

"The sh'pan—once the most valued objects on our planet," !Jng!xl said thoughtfully, moving around to the other side of the display case so that it was between her and Sylvie. The case held several dozen jewels—diamonds, they looked like to Sylvie—larger than any she had seen before, anywhere. "Two hundred years ago, they would have been worth the lives of every !xaka! on this island. Now"—the !xaka! made a motion that Sylvie supposed was the equivalent of a human shrug—"we make them by the ton."

!Jng!xl held up her clan badge, a black stone encrusted with five jewels just like the ones in the display case, for Sylvie to see.

"They're still beautiful," Sylvie said, trying to associate the symbol on the badge with a clan, and failing. That was odd. She thought she was familiar with all the major clans.

"They are indeed," !Jng!xl said. The !xaka! stopped examining the jewels and turned to face Sylvie directly. "I am surprised to see you here—the museum does not receive too many visitors."

"I only found it by accident," Sylvie said. "I got lost." Which was half-true; she'd come into N'Gossa simply to send off her story, but either Ho!xa had given her the wrong directions, or she had followed them incorrectly. After getting off the floatcar she'd found herself in the middle of a cluster of several large, ornate buildings, and the small comm station she was supposed to be looking for was nowhere in sight. She'd taken the opportunity to wander into this one, hoping to find someone who could help her get her bearings back. To her surprise, the soldiers on guard had accepted her press card without comment, and allowed her inside.

"The comm station is not far from here—I can show it to you easily," !Jng!xl said after she'd finished telling her story. "But as long as you've found the museum, you must let me show you some more of the exhibits here."

"I'd be delighted," Sylvie said, surprised by the offer. A lowly reporter such as herself would normally not have been permitted here. Surely this !Jng!xl knew that.

"It is my pleasure. We !xaka! are very proud of these exhibits from our past, and we have very few chances to show them off."

Sylvie followed her out into the hall, her holocams trailing a few meters behind, the o!xer ever further back. Everything here was so elaborately done-up, so ornate. The entranceways and halls between exhibits were all decorated with gleaming metal scrollwork and brilliantly colored panels of stone, showing an attention to detail that would have shamed a shri.

It was all in such great contrast to the cave she'd lived in for the last few weeks that it made her stop and think.

The G!at built this museum, with its fine and expensive decoration. And they built the workers' complex—with nothing but cave after cave dug out of the ground, the same size, the same shape, the same distance apart, as if someone had come along with a giant scoop and at carefully measured intervals dug out the prescribed amount of rock.

How a race could produce works of such beauty, and condemn the majority of their citizens to live in abject poverty. . . .

It was behind her.

But it would make good material for her next article.

She fingered the controls in her belt, and her holocams jetted ahead of her, recording the images in the hall in minute detail.

The data solids for her first article were in the back pocket of her jumpsuit. Her unauthorized visit to the G!at tower had gotten her all the confirmation of the coming clan war she needed—and much more: TV conversations regarding the weapons buildup, troop movements among the colony worlds, and even (to her delight) a stray word or two about Zeke's appearance before the Diet.

Of course, she couldn't put all those details in the article itself. The G!at, as she knew, were monitoring all outgoing transmissions. So she'd encoded them within an article on the taga!xi—not an uncontroversial subject, but certainly not one that would draw the G!at's attention the way details of their war preparations would.

And yet the article wasn't filler; she was proud of it, not only for what it said, but the conditions she'd written it under: conditions she considered unfit for living, conditions the taga!xi would spend their whole lives in— without complaint.

Another thing that was beyond her.

The taga!xi knew the vast wealth the G!at controlled. They saw the magnificent structures of the Keep, caught glimpses of the luxuriant life-styles the G!at rulers led. All were fruits of *their* labor. And all they could say was—

The G!at were the rulers; the G!at owned everything; the G!at were always right. It was the way things were.

Once, Sylvie had tried to draw Ho!xa out, get him to talk honestly about his masters. He'd simply refused.

"Sylvie Pharr—it would not be correct," he said. "To question the G!at—it would not be my place."

Sylvie hadn't become a reporter to preach. She'd had enough experience to know that there was more than one side to every story; too often, she'd seen the best-intended interference result in disaster. For the !xaka!, slavery was just business as usual, part of a long-established way of life. But there were other ways of life in the galaxy, and to her way of thinking, by joining the United Worlds, the !xaka! had become part of one of those other ways, had cracked open the door on that wider world.

Sylvie intended to kick that door down, and show Kadak!xa's clan what was on the other side.

Getting her article out would be just the first step, but it was important. Maybe as important as getting Zeke and Marty the details she'd encoded in her article.

"Ah," !Jng!xl said, interrupting her train of thought. "Here is an exhibit you should be most interested in."

They had come to a circular room, with a single display case in its center.

"The Scrolls of N'Gossa," !Jng!xl said, crossing to the exhibit, Sylvie a step behind. "They date back to the founding of N'Gossa—the first great civilization of Ahng. Our planet's greatest archaeological treasure."

The case contained more than a dozen metal tablets, laid out next to each other side by side, like the pages of a book. Each was inscribed with symbols that reminded Sylvie of hieroglyphs her father had once shown her. In the center of the display was a tablet twice as large as any of the others, and much more elaborately engraved.

"What do they say?" Sylvie asked. Her holocams moved forward and began recording the images over her shoulder.

"The smaller tablets are a listing of transactions and inventories," !Jng!xl responded. "Here." She ran a hand along the edge of the case next to one of the tablets, and blue writing appeared in the air above it. "A translation into the modern G!at language." She waved her hand over the edge of the case again, and the writing disappeared.

"And the larger tablet?" Sylvie asked. "What does that say?"

"Ah—this." A flick of her hand, and a much larger body of text appeared in the air. "The G!at *!x'kuta*—'the principles of order.' Written by the priests of ancient N'Gossa to establish their supremacy over all secular matters."

"The G!at?" Sylvie asked. "What do they have to do with it?"

"They are the descendants of that ancient priesthood—the sole remaining link to the first civilization on our planet."

Sylvie shook her head. She had a hard time thinking of the G!at as priests right about now.

"Of course, their religious convictions have long since given way to economic practicalities," !Jng!xl continued, "but the hierarchy established in this document carries over to the present day. Moreover, the G!at have used their association with the ancient N'Gossa to establish a position of superiority over the other clans."

"You don't sound as if you care for them very much."

!Jng!xl bowed. "You will forgive me if I decline any further comment on that, Sylvie Pharr. I am here now as a diplomat."

She smiled. She already had a pretty good idea of how the !xaka! would have commented further.

Sylvie set her holocams to capturing the Scrolls from every possible angle. She wanted to have a good series of images for Zeke when he arrived.

Finally, she finished, and turned away from the display case.

Just as a half-dozen other !xaka! entered the room.

U!xani, she knew instantly, the largest group of them she'd seen since Kadak!xa had been captured, but what—

!Jng!xl's two o!xer moved instantly aside.

Another !xaka!, resplendent in enough armor to coat a small spaceship, moved in front of the warriors.

"The holocams," she barked out. "Take them."

"Wait," Sylvie said. "Don't—"

Two of the u!xani moved forward and grabbed for Sylvie's holocams—which immediately jetted out of reach.

"Deactivate," the leader snapped.

One pulled out a hand-weapon and took aim. There was a short humming sound, a small flash of light—and the holocams fell to the floor.

"What did you do?" Sylvie asked, moving to recover her holocams.

The u!xani who had fired growled threateningly at her.

In an instant, !Jng!xl cut in front of Sylvie.

"Warrior," !Jng!xl hissed, in a voice suddenly harsh and threatening. "Would you harm my companion?"

"Councilor—forgiveness," the u!xani said, backing off and bowing.

The !xaka! who had given the order to capture Sylvie's holocams moved forward. "Councilor, you are aware of the regulations regarding the Scrolls."

!Jng!xl didn't move an inch. "As the regulation makes so little sense to me, Councilor, it had slipped my mind. Please accept my humblest apologies."

"And please accept ours for troubling your viewing of the exhibit, Councilor." The two faced each other for a moment without speaking, and Sylvie sensed a real animosity beneath their relatively civil exchange, as if this was just the latest installment in a long-running battle.

The newcomer turned to Sylvie.

"Obviously, you are here as the Councilor's companion, so I will not ask you to leave. I will, however, make you aware of our rules, as the Councilor has apparently not seen fit to do so. No images of the Scrolls may be taken—no copies of the Scrolls may be made. It is the law." With that, the !xaka! turned and left the room, the soldiers following.

Sylvie bent down and picked up her holocams.

"Trashed," she said in disgust. "Completely useless."

!Jng!xl shook her head. "I did not think they would trouble you, Sylvie Pharr—I am sorry."

"Not your fault," Sylvie shrugged. "Who was that— the one who gave the orders?"

"That? That was Vajix!krk—she is G!at Councilor to the Diet of Monopolistics." !Jng!xl practically spat the words.

Sylvie was impressed.

"She called you Councilor as well."

"I am the in!chi representative to the Diet," !Jng!xl acknowledged.

Sylvie frowned. No wonder she hadn't recognized the symbol on !Jng!xl's clan badge—she'd never heard of the in!chi.

"I don't want to seem insulting," she said, "but—"

"No insult taken, Sylvie Pharr," !Jng!xl cut her off, apparently having recognized her difficulty. "Those of my clan do not often interact with off-world species. We are what you might call brokers—though more precisely, we provide neutral ground, where each clan may stockpile its funds, or exchange its goods for those of the others, exacting a small fee for our services."

"Neutral ground?" Sylvie asked. "Is that truly necessary?"

!Jng!xl nodded. "Unfortunately, it is. The other clans have a regrettable tendency to fight among

themselves. Our embassies are recognized as safe ter-
ritory during any such battles."

"Battles?" Sylvie frowned. "You mean here—on
Ahng?" The idea hadn't occurred to her that the wars
planned for the colony worlds might actually spread
to the !xaka! home planet.

"Oh, yes, though the last war on this planet was—"
she paused a moment "—not quite fifty years ago. Over
twenty million !xaka! perished."

Sylvie, stunned, said nothing.

!Jng!xl motioned her o!xer forward. "Allow them to
assist you in cleaning up. I must be going—the Diet meets
in half an hour. It was a pleasure to meet you, Sylvie
Pharr. I hope to see you again soon."

Sylvie smiled. "I hope so too. You're the first person—
!xaka!—I've really been able to talk with here."

"I usually come to the museum at this time every day,
between sessions. Why don't you meet me at the entrance
outside—tomorrow, perhaps?"

"It's a date," Sylvie said. She truly was looking forward
to talking a lot more with the Councilor—not only about
what was in the museum, but about what was going on
outside it.

!Jng!xl bowed slightly. "Until then, Sylvie Pharr."

"Until then, Councilor." Sylvie squatted down by the
wreckage of her holocams—and felt the data solids in the
pocket of her coverall press against her leg.

"Oh—Councilor!"

!Jng!xl turned.

"The comm station—you were going to show me
where it was."

"I'm afraid I don't have time at this moment. Perhaps you will let one of my o!xer take you."

Sylvie smiled. "I was hoping you'd say that."

"Will I see you tomorrow at the museum?" the Councilor asked.

Sylvie nodded. "Tomorrow at the museum."

Shoving the ruined holocams into her bag, she followed the o!xer out of the museum.

Chapter Six

Zeke woke slowly. He had been dreaming, and in his dream he had made an important discovery. Now he couldn't remember what it was. Something to do with Sir Arthur Evans and—no, that wasn't it. It was something to do with the !xaka! . . . wasn't it?"

Damn. The more awake he got, the more it slipped away.

He lay still for a moment, trying to drift off to sleep again and call the memory back—but it was no use.

The transparent shell around him recessed back, and he sat up.

On either side of him, deepsleep pods were opening. Marty appeared from the one on his right.

"I'm hungry," he announced.

"What a surprise," Zeke said. He sat up. "Herb?"

A few seconds passed as a low thrum of power coursed through the ship.

"Right here, Zeke." Herb's voice issued from the speakers in the *Ostrom*'s hull.

"How'd we come through IO?"

"Checking now . . ."

"I really hate this, Doc." Jackson sat up slowly and yawned, rubbing the back of his neck. "I never know if I'll wake up in one piece."

He smiled to let Zeke know he was joking, but his concern was genuine—and understandable. The IO drive process was never 100 percent successful. If they were lucky, neither the ship or any of them had been damaged in any important way.

Reelys emerged from the pod to Marty's right and floated immediately toward the ceiling, twisting to bask every part of his'er body in the light. S'he, too, must be hungry—for shri were photosynthetic.

"System integrity at 99.999 percent," Herb announced. "A few backup circuits have malfunctioned, but whether from the transition to invariance overdrive or simple old age, I cannot say."

"Old age?" Marty asked. "How long were we out?"

"Exactly forty-eight years, seven months, six days," Herb replied instantly. "IO switchover occurred seven hours ago—on Ahng, it is now approximately fourteen days since you left Sylvie behind."

Reelys floated down to join his'er companions. "But this is the third such journey the *Ostrom* has made recently—so the circuits in question are actually over a century and a half old."

As was everything else on the ship that hadn't spent that hundred and fifty years in deepsleep, Zeke added silently. Yet in the world outside, no time had passed—thanks to the IO drive. Engaging the IO initiated an instantaneous annihilation/reannihilation of every particle of matter on the ship—effectively cancelling the passage of time outside the ship's frame of reference.

Still, the two weeks had gone by on Ahng. That was a long time.

"Two weeks," Zeke said aloud. "A lot can happen in two weeks. When will we be in range for radio contact?"

"Another few hours," Herb told him. "Half a day till we reach Ahng."

He nodded. "All right, then. Half an hour from now—in the main lab."

"I'll synchronize my watch," Marty said sarcastically. "In the meantime, I'm getting something to eat."

"I thought you said all the food on board was gone," Jackson said, glaring at him.

Marty smiled innocently. "Did I say that?"

The two left the room.

"Something is troubling you, Ezekiel," Reelys said after Marty and Jackson were gone.

"You're right," Zeke said, clambering out of the sleep pod. "I don't like going into this cold." He clasped his hands behind his back and began to pace. "We don't know what's been going on for the past two weeks; the G!at have had all this time to prepare their strategy, and our claim could be heard and dismissed in less time than it takes to—"

"We will know something soon enough," Reelys interrupted, jetting directly into Zeke's path so he had to stop pacing. "And I have studied the procedural rules the Diet operates under. There are no tricks the G!at will be able to try I cannot counter. Our claim *will* be heard. And even if it is dismissed, we have discussed several options—"

"I know all that," Zeke admitted "I guess I'm just a little nervous."

"Nervous?" Reelys asked. "Ezekiel, I've known you long enough to know that you do not just get 'nervous.'" The shri jetted closer. "What is really troubling you?"

Zeke shoved his hands into the pockets of his coverall, and paced away in the other direction.

It was funny—he'd always been a loner, from the time he was a boy right up through his Academy days, always more concerned with following his own interests than fitting into a group. Really, he'd never found any group worth fitting into. Then he'd joined the Legion of Ares—an army of mercenaries, of mavericks, of people who didn't belong anywhere else. Just like him. Reelys, and Marty, and Jackson. . . .

And Sylvie.

And now they all belonged someplace.

"I can't help thinking about Sylvie—alone on that planet," he began, turning back to face Reelys.

"She is more than capable of handling herself," the shri said gently. "You know that better than I do. And certainly the G!at would do nothing to harm her—not unless they wanted to bring the wrath of the United Worlds down on themselves. Not to mention your own esteemable wrath."

Zeke smiled. "And a lot of really bad publicity. I know all that, Reelys. It's just that when it comes to Sylvie. . . ." his voice trailed off.

"Yes?" Reelys prompted.

"Well, I guess I—" Zeke stopped, thinking about the fight they'd had before she left, and started again. "You know, she and I never talk much, but sometimes I think that we—"

"Zeke," Herb's voice came over the speakers again. "I'm picking up the echoes of a transmission from Ahng—UCI frequency."

"Sylvie," Zeke said, smiling and slapping his hand against the side of the pod. "Tell Marty and Jackson to meet me in the main lab—"

"They're on their way, too," Herb replied—but Zeke was already out the door, Reelys a few meters behind.

The *Ostrom*, like almost all spaceships, basically flew itself, so there was no need for a cockpit, or a bridge, or any such flight control center. All operations could be controlled from anywhere by simply telling the ship—actually, by telling Herb—what to do.

Because of that, whatever crew was aboard tended to gather in the largest and most comfortable room—the main lab—for meetings. In addition to being a fully equipped, state-of-the-art archaeological laboratory that many governments couldn't match, the main lab also had the largest videoscreen on the ship—it took up an entire four-meter-square wall.

When Zeke and Reelys walked in, Marty and Jackson were already sitting in two chairs in front of the videoscreen. Sylvie Pharr was on it.

"She just started, Zeke. This is the unscrambled feed for UCI," Marty said. Zeke pulled up a chair next to them.

"—where they have lived here for countless generations, while behind me—"

Sylvie was standing next to a group of !xaka!, most of whom were trying not to be noticed—which was very un-!xaka!-like behavior. These !xaka! weren't wearing any armor, or jewelry, and carried themselves differently, less arrogantly than most others Zeke had known. And now that he was looking, they even looked a little different—maybe the middle two segments were proportionally larger, the ring of muscle between them more developed. . . .

Stop playing scientist, he told himself.

He turned his attention to Sylvie.

She looked a little worse for the wear. Her hair (which was normally immaculately styled in what Zeke thought of as a Cleopatra cut) she had simply brushed back from her face, and the red jumpsuit she was wearing looked wrinkled.

"She looks like hell," Marty offered.

"Yeah," Jackson said.

"She looks fine," Zeke countered. "Just a little tired."

Sylvie was a good reporter—maybe the best UCI had, and this piece was no exception. It ran ten minutes, and when it was over, the lab was silent for several seconds.

"Wow," Jackson said. "The lady pulled no punches."

"Indeed," Reelys added thoughtfully. "And this is to be the first of several, she said."

Zeke nodded. Once the G!at saw this, they would not be too happy with Sylvie Pharr.

"Lights on, Herb," Zeke ordered, standing. "Did we get it?"

"Having trouble isolating the scrambled track," Herb said. Sylvie had transmitted her article in one highly compressed burst of data—the picture, the sound, everything—and before Marty left Ahng two weeks ago, the two of them had agreed on a numerical progression for a second audio channel within her article, a progression that would translate as signal noise to anyone else. It was that scrambled channel Herb was trying to find.

"Are you sure about that progression, Marty?" Herb asked.

"Of course I'm sure."

"Give it to him again," Zeke said.

Marty snapped off a series of six-digit numbers.

Herb was silent for a full minute.

"There's nothing there, Zeke," he said finally.

"Nothing?"

"Maybe she just didn't have time to send a message," Jackson offered.

"Maybe."

Marty shook his head. "She must have found out something."

"Then," Jackson began hesitantly, "maybe they found the scrambled message and erased it."

They all turned to him.

"How would they find out about the second audio channel?" Zeke asked.

"Theoretically, it would not be difficult," Reelys said. "Once they started looking. . . ."

"If we assume 'they' are the G!at," Jackson added, "there were a lot of good reasons to look over Sylvie's article very closely."

"Indeed," Reelys continued. "If we consider the fact that Sylvie's article was designed to cause the G!at genuine embarrassment, and that she planned several more of them—"

"Yeah—so?" Marty asked.

Zeke knew where Reelys was heading.

"What Reelys is trying to tell you," Zeke said, "is that we may find ourselves bargaining with the G!at for more than one prisoner."

A stricken look crossed Marty's face.

"Sylvie?"

Zeke nodded. "It's quite possible they've got her too."

"You've got it, Ho!xa," Sylvie said. "Now just remember—follow me."

The two of them were in Sylvie's cave, preparing to film the proceedings of the Diet this afternoon. Ho!xa was going to be her assistant, and he was very nervous about this new role.

Right now he was walking behind her, about two meters, just like she'd told him. Only he was pointing the holocam into the ground.

"No, no—aim the scanner over my shoulder," she said, laughing. She grabbed onto the holocam he held and placed it in the correct position. She'd been very lucky—she'd been able to cobble together one working holocam out of the three the G!at soldiers had broken in the museum. Working as in recording—but not as in ambulatory. Either she would have to hold it, or someone else would—and why not Ho!xa?

He grabbed the holocam back from Sylvie, and resumed his station two meters behind her, this time holding the holocam at the right angle. It looked like a toy in his hands.

Sylvie smiled. Considering how eager Ho!xa was to assume his new role, it was hard to believe how strongly he had opposed the idea at first.

"Sylvie Pharr—it is not permitted for a slave to observe the Diet in session," he had said.

"You wouldn't be an observer!" Sylvie replied. "You'd be my holocamperson—holocam!xaka!, in this case."

He thought about that for a moment.

"The G!at will never allow it," Ho!xa insisted.

"They won't have a choice," Sylvie said. "You'll be UCI staff—not under their jurisdiction." And she herself was going under !Jng!xl's protection.

Ho!xa had remained silent.

Sylvie had kept on arguing. "I'm offering you a chance to see your sister again," she said. "You talked about how lucky she was to have me as a friend. You're her brother, and this may be her—"

Ho!xa bowed his head, ducking away from her.

Suddenly Sylvie had realized what a difficult thing she was asking him to do. It was easy for her to talk about doing the "right" thing—but a lot harder for someone who had lived his whole life one way to do a complete about-face.

"Ho!xa," she had begun again, more gently—but he had immediately interrupted her.

"I will go," he said in a small voice—it was funny, she didn't know a !xaka! could talk in a small voice, but that's just what it was—"Sylvie Pharr, I will go," he repeated, stronger this time. "But you must show me how to use this—holocam?"

Then she had laughed, and told him what to do. Which basically involved just carrying the holocam, but even so, his new responsibility had made him nervous and excited.

Sylvie was nervous and excited too. Nervous, because today she would know whether or not Kadak!xa would be free, or a slave to the G!at for the rest of her life.

And excited, because Zeke and the *Ostrom* were here.

"They entered our space two hours ago," !Jng!xl had told her, after they'd met at the museum again yesterday. "We will hear their claim on the slave tomorrow."

Sylvie had been surprised to hear of Zeke's arrival through a third party—she had expected him to contact her directly, to respond through Kadak!xa's family to the message she'd hidden in her article. Most likely, they were afraid they couldn't find a secure channel. She'd hate to think of him walking unaware into the middle of a Diet preparing for war.

A sudden flurry of motion in the tunnel caught her attention.

Two huge G!at u!xani appeared in the entranceway to her cave. They were armored in the same fashion as those she had seen in the museum—they might even have been two of the same ones.

"Sylvie Pharr," one began without preamble. "We have been sent by the Supreme Councilor to escort you to today's proceedings of the Diet of Monopolistics."

"I don't need any escort," Sylvie said, rising to her feet. What was this all about? "My assistant and I are perfectly capable of making our way to the proceedings unaccompanied. You can just go and tell the Supreme Councilor that for me."

Neither of them moved.

"I see no assistant," the u!xani said, staring straight at Ho!xa. The smaller !xaka! visibly flinched and backed into the corner of the cave.

"There," Sylvie said, pointing to Ho!xa. "He is my assistant."

The two warriors exchanged glances, then one moved forward and ripped Sylvie's holocam out of Ho!xa's grasp.

"Hey," Sylvie said. "What are you doing?"

"This is your holocam?" the u!xani asked.

"Yes, but—"

Not waiting for Sylvie to finish, the soldier folded it in half, as if it were a piece of cardboard, and flung it against the cave wall—missing Ho!xa by inches.

"I believe your holocam is broken," the u!xani said.

"You bastard." Sylvie swore without thinking—then realized that, in this status-conscious society, she had given just about the worst insult possible.

And the warrior she'd spoken to realized it too. She hiss/click!ed angrily, and advanced.

Ho!xa moved in front of her.

"No!" Sylvie screamed. "They won't hurt me—Ho!xa!"

The u!xani—half again as big as Ho!xa—hissed again. Then, without warning, she moved—faster than Sylvie would have thought possible—slamming into Ho!xa, carrying him to the cave floor.

Sylvie thought she felt the ground shake. One of them screamed. There was a horrible smell, like burning acid.

"Ho!xa!" Sylvie cried out.

Suddenly, the two stopped fighting.

The u!xani was the first to rise.

"What is happening?" the warrior asked.

Sylvie didn't know what she meant at first. Then she realized the ground really was shaking, rumbling beneath her feet.

"Earthquake," she said softly. Another tremor—like the one that had ruptured the tunnel two weeks ago.

The two warriors glanced around, suddenly nervous and unsure of themselves.

Sylvie knelt down by Ho!xa, who lay still on the ground.

He rolled over slowly, and reached for her.

There was a great gash in his side, and horrible burns covered half of his body.

"Sylvie Pharr—" he croaked, his mandibles working weakly back and forth.

Then the world fell apart.

This was no mere tremor—it was a full-fledged earthquake. The tunnel bent and twisted like a corkscrew, the ground thrust up at crazy angles.

One soldier was thrown heavily against the other. They tumbled to the cave floor—and disappeared without a sound into a crack in the earth, a crack that closed as suddenly as it had appeared.

The ground buckled again, throwing Ho!xa into the cave wall. He screamed once—and the ground folded around him, silencing his cries and snatching him away from view.

Sylvie reeled backward, trying to run away.

But there was nowhere to run.

The cave floor lifted beneath her feet again, and slammed her against something hard. There was an instant of excruciating pain.

And then nothing.

Chapter Seven

Marty had an uncomfortable sense of déjà vu as he felt the *Ostrom* dock with the shuttle station. In his mind, he replayed the G!at's underhanded seizure of Kadak!xa, and their detention of Sylvie and himself. Now they had told the *Ostrom* and her crew that preparations had been made for them to appear before the Diet.

But he'd be damned if he was going to get caught flat-footed again.

Not that he didn't trust the plan Reelys and Zeke had come up with; it had gotten them this far, after all, and looked like it was going to get them in to talk to the G!at. But they were banking a little too heavily on the G!at behaving sensibly, predictably. Reelys kept talking about their being bound by custom, but as far as he could tell, what the G!at were bound by was greed—for money and power. And that made for unpredictable behavior.

On the other hand, maybe Zeke was right. Maybe he just disliked the fact that Reelys was such a know-it-all. In the Legion, where his'er main function had been to serve as their intelligence agent on the various worlds their assignments took them to, Reelys had never found a subject s/he couldn't speak on . . . and on . . . and on. . . .

He clenched and unclenched his hands into fists, waiting for the airlock to cycle.

"Easy." Zeke stood next to him, arms folded tightly across the front of his cold-suit, and managed a tight-lipped smile. "You act like you're expecting them to capture us."

Marty refused to relax. He stared at the door straight ahead of him, waiting for it to open. "They're welcome to try," he said.

There was a sudden hiss of air—then the door slid back, and they were looking out onto the corridor of the shuttle station.

The four of them moved out of the airlock, Zeke first, followed by Marty and Jackson, then Reelys, who stayed back, hovering next to their gear.

The *Ostrom* cycled shut behind them.

"Ezekiel Bones."

Marty turned—and suddenly, he had that uncomfortable sense of déjà vu again.

Standing in front of them was the same huge !xaka! that had given Sylvie and him such a hard time before.

Zeke stepped forward.

"I am Dr. Ezekiel Bones."

"A shuttle has been prepared for your use," the !xaka! told Zeke. She peered closely at Marty, as if she recognized him. "Your escort will be along shortly."

Marty shouldered his way forward. He was in no mood for any red tape right now. "Just tell us where it is—or don't such requests fall within your area of responsibility?"

The !xaka! growled. "Two berths over to your right—even a *hlidjski* could not miss it."

Marty was about to say something else—then Reelys jetted in front of him, a brilliant flash of color, his'er body inflated to impressive size.

"We are anxious to proceed," s/he said imperiously. "If you could show us to the shuttle, we would be most obliged."

The !xaka! shrank visibly. "Forgiveness, honored guests. This way, please," she said, backing away, careful to keep her head low, averting her gaze from Reelys.

Marty winked at Zeke. Amazing what a simple, politely phrased request could do—especially when it came from a member of the one race !xaka! considered their betters.

"You see, Marty," Reelys said, moving alongside him. "It is exactly as I told you. You would benefit from a closer study of the !xaka! caste system yourself. For instance, they normally consider hlidjski to be of a status just slightly higher than slaves, since you were genetically engineered for a specific purpose. However, if you were to inform them that you were an ex-Legionnaire, thus a soldier, you would move up the ladder. . . ."

Marty began counting in his head. By the time he reached forty-eight, they were in their shuttle, strapped down and ready to take off. He chose a window seat, as far away from Reelys as he could get. Thankfully, they all passed the ride in silence.

From space, Ahng shone like polished ivory, an unblemished, perfectly white sphere. The planet was coated with ice; what few surface features it had— scattered island chains, a few larger landmasses, none even as big as Great Britain—were barely visible through the shuttle windows.

As they circled in closer, the first traces of civilization began to appear—dark patches amid the light, evidence of the planet's monumental cities.

A blanket of clouds rose up before the shuttle, obscuring Marty's view of the planet below.

He turned in his seat. Across from him, Zeke was staring out the window, his eyes unseeing, his expression unreadable. Jackson was sleeping. Reelys was busy reading something off a small display screen. An eyestalk bent and peered up at Marty for a second, then dipped back down to study the screen.

He thought about asking the shri what s/he was reading, but decided he would probably know soon enough.

Suddenly, the light from Ahng's sun streamed through the window—and there, looming before them, was N'Gossa Island, and the Keep.

Jackson sat up, rubbed his eyes. He leaned over Marty and looked out his window.

"Is that it? Is that N'Gossa?"

"You bet," Marty said. "Next stop, worm world."

"Marty," Reelys began. "It would be inaccurate to refer to the !xaka! as worms—although they superficially resemble them, their internal structure. . . ."

Marty groaned softly, and turned back to the window.

Ahng was cold.

From his'er studies, Reelys knew the average surface temperature during the day was fifty below centigrade, and almost twice that cold at night. Life had evolved here only because the oceans beneath the ice were warmed by the volcanic processes within the planet itself. Not even the !xaka! could survive unprotected on the surface for long.

The humans had cold-suits built to handle that kind of temperature (theoretically—Ezekiel had mentioned that they'd never had the chance to test them in conditions so extreme), but Reelys certainly didn't. Thankfully, the !xaka! preferred things a little warmer themselves; inside both the shuttle station where they landed and the float-car they were now riding in, the temperature felt closer to twenty above—not as warm as Reelys would have preferred, but comfortable enough.

The shuttle station was on a smaller island just off the coast of N'Gossa. As the floatcar journeyed across the short strait of ice separating the two (a little too fast to suit the shri's taste), Reelys had his'er first glimpse of the Keep.

S/he was none too impressed.

The !xaka! fondness for unnecessary ornament carried over into their buildings—as did their natural disregard for aesthetics. Overall, the G!at city was a textbook example of unchecked, unplanned, and ultimately unattractive growth.

Zeke, too, watched, wondering where among the forbidding jungle of towers his missing friends were—and if something had happened to Sylvie because of the article she'd filed. So far, they had been unable to raise her, or Ho!xa, from the *Ostrom*.

"Do you think this Great Hall we're supposed to go to is one of those towers?" Jackson asked.

"Probably," Zeke nodded.

"The ugliest one," Marty added.

"On the contrary," Reelys said. "It is not a tower at all." S/he raised a tentacle and pointed.

The floatcar had circled the vastness of the Keep, and was even now coming into view of a single huge building, one that, despite its relatively low height, dominated this entire sector of the city.

As they drew closer, they could see the building was surrounded by a clear plastic dome. A section of that dome now lifted, and the floatcar descended within.

"The Great Hall," Reelys announced, as they landed.

The area beneath the dome was a single huge plaza; directly in front of them, occupying most of that plaza, stood a massive, square edifice, built entirely of identical blocks of dull black stone, or perhaps metal. A thousand meters long, another fifty high, it dwarfed both them and the columns of !xaka! standing in front of it. A series of intricate designs, etched directly into the surface, ran the length of the building's facade, from twenty meters above their heads to the start of the roof. It reminded Zeke of nothing so much as one of the colossal structures of Imperial Rome—the buildings encircling it, indeed almost the entire city, seemed to have been built around this place.

"Wow," Jackson said, "*Great* is the word for it, all right."

Zeke nodded silently, and leaned against the floatcar window to study the Hall more closely.

Reelys's mouthstalk settled gently on his shoulder.

"Imagine, Ezekiel," the shri said softly. "You are looking at a piece of this planet's history, a remnant of fabled N'Gossa itself."

"I thought the original city had been entirely destroyed," Zeke said, turning back over his shoulder to talk to the shri.

Reelys lifted his'er mouthstalk, and floated up next to Zeke. "So legend had it. But the same G!at scientists who discovered the Scrolls uncovered the ruins of that great city—including several of the building stones from the original Great Hall. Those stones served as both template and foundation for this replica."

"It may be a replica," Zeke said thoughtfully. "But it's still the most impressive-looking building in the Keep."

"As it was built to be," Reelys said. "It has served as the meeting place of the Diet of Monopolistics for close to a century."

Zeke nodded. Reelys's mention of the Scrolls had brought those forbidden documents to mind again—and he determined to at least ask the G!at for permission to examine them.

As they spoke, the top of the floatcar lifted around them, letting in a crisp, cool breeze that reminded Zeke of autumn. The breeze also carried with it a somewhat metallic scent—a smell Zeke had grown to associate with the !xaka! during his years in the Legion.

He turned and caught Marty sniffing as well.

"They still stink," the hlidjski muttered under his breath.

Zeke shook his head, and swiveled back in his seat to face Jackson, who seemed less concerned with how the planet smelled than how it looked. His head was tilted as far back as it could go, and he was staring up at the Great Hall, and the dome that now rose all around them.

Outside the dome, looming over the Great Hall like a series of forty-story sentinels, stood a half-dozen obelisk-shaped towers. No windows marred their smooth, sandy-colored surfaces; the only ornamentation was a series of panels on each, stretching around the obelisks just above the dome line. Each tower bore a different pattern. As Zeke looked closer, he also saw passageways leading from the domed plaza they were now in into each of the towers.

"What are those things?" Jackson asked, pointing up at one of the obelisks.

"Consular towers, belonging to each of the major clans," Reelys answered. "Note the clan-symbols—the soldiers wear them as well."

"Those are all soldiers?" Marty asked. Hundreds of !xaka! lined the approach to the Great Hall itself, and surrounded the entranceways to the consular towers. Each was heavily armored, particularly around the soft !xaka! underbelly, with clan designations brilliantly emblazoned on their chest protectors. Each also carried a number of small weapons in a harness that hung from their bodies.

Zeke nodded and leaned closer to him. "I hope none of them heard you saying how much they stink."

Marty gave him a sour look.

"It is strange to see so many soldiers," Reelys said slowly. S/he drew an eyestalk back from the window and turned it up to peer at Zeke. "We may be facing a slightly more explosive situation than I previously thought."

"'Slightly more explosive?'" Marty asked. "What does that mean?"

"All these soldiers aren't usually here, is that right?" Zeke asked.

"This is my first time here as well, Ezekiel—but, yes, my studies indicate that only in times of great unrest is such full-scale mobilization of the clan armies done, even for ceremonial purposes." Reelys exhaled thoughtfully, and turned his'er eyestalk to study the columns of soldiers again.

"Maybe we could come back another time," Marty suggested.

Zeke glared at him.

Two !xaka!, wearing the G!at clan symbol, moved forward and helped them disembark from the floatcar.

"These are o!xer," Reelys told Zeke quietly. "Bureaucrats. Clerical workers, for the most part."

"Forgiveness—Ezekiel Bones?" one of them asked in universal pidgin.

Zeke nodded.

"We are to escort you into the Great Hall. Please surrender your weapons."

"We don't have any weapons," Zeke said.

"No weapons?" The !xaka! looked back to her companion, who clicked her mandibles together loudly.

"They do not believe you," Reelys said.

The two G!at moved forward.

"We must insist—it is the law."

Zeke stepped aside to allow Reelys to confront them.

"Where," Reelys thundered, "would I hide weapons?"

The two o!xer immediately bent their heads low to the ground.

Zeke smothered a laugh. Jackson and Marty smiled.

"Forgiveness, honored guests—but it is the law."

"The search will not be necessary," Reelys said. "Inform your masters we are here."

Apparently deciding that discretion was the better part of valor in this instance, the o!xer complied, backing away and disappearing into the Great Hall.

"Now what do we do?" Marty asked.

"We wait," Zeke said.

"Maybe we should try and contact Sylvie again."

Zeke shook his head.

"One thing at a time," he said softly. "One at a time."

A few minutes later, another o!xer—a different clan, Zeke noticed—returned.

"You will now be escorted before the Diet."

"I guess they don't want *my* weapons," Jackson whispered, falling into step beside Zeke.

They were led beneath the open entranceway of the Great Hall, a portal large enough to march a dozen elephants through side-by-side, and down a series of long, curving corridors. Soldiers bristling with armament lined the corridors at regular intervals, as did various decorative wall panels and sculptures.

Finally, they came to a large circular doorway, easily twenty feet tall. The o!xer motioned them forward. The door panels irised open like a flower unfolding, and they were facing the Diet of Monopolistics.

The Great Hall had been well named. The building was one room—a room the size of a small sporting arena, which it somewhat resembled. Columns of soldiers stood in neat, orderly ranks on the main floor, their backs to the door through which Zeke and the others had just entered. Along either side of the room there were seating galleries, sectioned off and separated at intervals by more soldiers. A great dais stood at the opposite end of the room from them—and more soldiers surrounded that.

"I'm impressed," Marty whispered.

"Are all of these guys in the Diet?" Jackson asked.

"In a manner of speaking, yes," Reelys answered, "though the only ones who need concern us are there, at the far end of the room. They comprise the Supreme Council. The chamber as a whole votes only on motions they approve—and any one of them owns the power of absolute veto on every motion raised."

"How do they ever get anything done?" Marty asked.

"A good question," Reelys said slowly. "I have begun to think that, whenever a truly important issue comes up, they go to war to decide it."

Marty stared at him'er. "That's not funny."

"*Come forward.*" The voice echoed in the Hall around him, and it was only when one of the soldiers motioned to him that Zeke realized the disembodied voice was talking to him.

Zeke stepped ahead, motioning his friends to follow. The soldiers on the main floor parted to allow them to pass through.

A hundred yards away, the Hall ended in a dais towering ten meters above the floor. The front of it was a deep blue; smooth and unblemished, like a monolithic gemstone. Atop the dais stretched a raised glass platform. Six !xaka! lay behind that platform, their clan symbols set in the walls behind them, dominating the Great Hall with their presence, an all-powerful council of judges.

Reelys recognized many of the same clans with whom he'd negotiated on Sersic-4. There were the !seri, Ghi!reeli, !van, !xamini, and of course the G!at—and one Councilor who seemed somehow apart from the others, whose clan symbol Reelys failed to recognize.

They had approached to within five meters of the dais when a soldier motioned for them to stop.

"Silence!" ordered the G!at Councilor, positioned in the middle of the six. "The Supreme Council will now—"

"A moment, Councilor." It was the !xaka! on the far right. "I ask Ezekiel Bones to identify his companions."

"Surely this is unimportant, the Ghi!reeli stated. "Can we not hear the human's claim quickly—and then move on to more important matters?"

Ezekiel stepped forward before any other !xaka! could speak. "Councilors—I am privileged to introduce my companions," he said, and Reelys was pleased, because he had warned Zeke not to let the Council dissolve into petty squabbling. "This is Marty Szigmond, Jackson Charles, and this"—he nodded—"is Reelys."

"Reelys," the !xaka! on the far right said. "Also known as Ahnast Jhiilla—formerly of the Galactic Council?"

"That is true."

A confused babble of clicks erupted from the other councilors.

"Thank you," the !xaka! said. "You may proceed with the claim, Councilor."

"A moment—before we begin," the G!at Councilor stated. "I wish to say that we are honored to have as guests of the Diet the noble shri Ahnast Jhiilla, Ezekiel Bones, and companions. No matter what our decision today, we hold them all in the highest respect."

"What the heck is that all about?" Marty asked.

"I believe," Reelys said, "I am being wooed, as the saying goes. Most interesting."

Zeke wondered if they'd suddenly gained another bargaining chip.

"We are here to decide the matter of service of the slave Kadak!xa," the G!at Councilor began. "Bring the slave forward."

To either side of the dais was a series of doorways. One of these opened—and two soldiers led another !xaka! out.

It was Kadak!xa.

She looked weak, the normal bronze of her carapace slightly faded. Seeing her again reminded Zeke of Sylvie. He turned and scanned the galleries on the sides of the Hall for her, but saw nothing. Had the G!at imprisoned her after seeing her article? If not, where was she?

He shoved those thoughts to the back of his mind, and faced the Diet again.

"You have laid claim to this slave, who is recorded as property of the G!at," the !xaka! continued.

"I have," Zeke acknowledged.

"You are prepared to speak for your claim?"

"I am."

"I will speak for the G!at," the !xaka! said. "By law, I must relinquish the chair. !Xa!xon of the Ghi!reeli will now preside."

The !xaka! on her immediate left rose.

"Councilor!" the !xaka! at the far left end of the table protested. "By custom, the new chair should be elected by a vote of the Diet at large."

The !van councilor," Reelys said in his ear. "Their power and influence has increased the last few years, while that of the G!at has declined. The two form the major power blocs."

"!Xa!xon is most senior," the first !xaka! said. "She will preside."

The other did not move. "I must protest."

"Councilors!" A third among the six rose. "A compromise suggestion."

The two exchanged suspicious glances, then nodded.

"I shall preside."

"Acceptable," the !van said instantly.

The G!at took a moment longer. "Acceptable—be it so noted. !Jng!xl of the in!chi shall preside."

"The in!chi?" Zeke asked Reelys.

"Power brokers—the closest thing Ahng has to a neutral clan, though they of course have their own interests," Reelys said thoughtfully. "I have never seen them before, though I believe I have heard them mentioned—including this !Jng!xl."

"Ezekiel Bones will now speak," !Jng!xl said.

He cleared his throat, and tried to remember everything he and Reelys had talked about before.

"I base my claim on the *vir'kash* paid by the Bones Energy Corporation to the slave Kadak!xa," he said.

He caught Kadak!xa's eye and tried to smile. "These payments have been documented and are a matter of record."

"The documents have been received and authenticated," the !van Councilor acknowledged.

The G!at Councilor shifted uncomfortably.

"Proceed," !Jng!xl instructed.

"No matter that the slave escaped from previous servitude, the fact remains that these payments form a real and binding contract between the slave and BEC. The Councilors will note the amount of payment rendered far exceeds that invested by the G!at. We have developed and trained the slave over a period of years at a substantial investment. Our claim is stronger, and should be binding."

"Well done, Ezekiel," Reelys said.

"Vajik!krk will now speak for the G!at," !Jng!xl said.

The G!at Councilor remained on the dais, staring down at Zeke as she spoke.

"Your claim is based on the services provided to the Bones Energy Corporation by the slave. You have documented this claim by producing records of payments rendered to the slave. How was the amount of payment to be rendered decided?"

"The payment is standard for all BEC employees," Zeke answered.

"How do these employees indicate their acceptance of this rate of payment?"

"A signed contract," Zeke said.

"Did the slave sign one of these contracts?"

"Yes."

"I see." Vajik!krk turned toward !Jng!xl. "Councilor, I move the human's claim be dismissed, and the G!at's given precedence."

"On what grounds?" the !van Councilor demanded, rising.

"One cannot, of course, have contracts with a slave," Vajik!krk said. "It is a fact."

On either side of the Great Hall, those !xaka! in the galleries stirred. The !van Councilor lowered herself again.

"It is a fact," !Jng!xl concurred. "The claim by Ezekiel Bones is hereby declared void. The slave is to be remanded into the custody of the G!at."

"Wait a minute," Zeke began. "You can't—"

"There is ample precedence for such a decision, Ezekiel Bones," !Jng!xl said. "Take the slave away," she ordered.

Kadak!xa erupted in fury as the soldiers seized her again, uttering a stream of curses Zeke couldn't begin to understand.

Zeke turned away from her.

"Reelys?" he asked.

The shri spoke in his ear. "I believe we have no other choice now. It is time to play our—what did you call it, Ezekiel?—trump card."

Zeke nodded, and turned back to the dais.

"I invoke the right of challenge," he said.

The !xaka! on the dais before them immediately broke into a confused babble. Those in the galleries exploded into a symphony of clicks.

It was almost a minute before !Jng!xl could silence them all.

"The challenge is an archaic custom, long out-of-date," she said.

"But still operative, I believe, Councilor," Zeke stood his ground.

"The human is correct." This from the !van Councilor. "The challenge has been issued—it must be answered."

"Or," !Jng!xl said. "The claim refuted."

Vajik!krk trembled in barely suppressed fury.

"The challenge," she said finally, "is accepted. Single combat—"

"Single combat," Zeke concurred, not lifting his gaze from that of Vajik!krk's.

"—to the death."

Chapter Eight

Jackson studied the Diet Supreme Council closely. A !xaka!'s compound eyes were incapable of the kind of contraction and expansion a human's were, and their features were nowhere near as mobile or expressive. But even with humans, facial expression alone couldn't tell you what someone was thinking—body language, smell, tone of voice, and half-a-dozen other things came into play, *if* you paid close enough attention.

Right now, Jackson was paying very close attention to the !xaka!.

The G!at Councilor—Vajix!krk—was very upset.

The in!chi Councilor was surprised—and somewhat upset.

The !van Councilor, who had previously been upset, was now smugly satisfied.

The Ghi!reeli Councilor was either somewhat satisfied, somewhat upset, or simply very hard to read.

!Jng!xl rose. "The challenge has been invoked. Each side must now designate a champion. Vajix!krk?"

The G!at Councilor descended from the dais and proceeded across the floor of the Great Hall to a column of soldiers, who visibly straightened as she passed. She walked back and forth, surveying the column twice, then stopped in front of the biggest, ugliest !xaka! Jackson had ever seen.

"Here is my champion," Vajix!krk stated.

A cacophony of wild noise—the !xaka! equivalent of applause, he supposed—burst from the other soldiers. The soldier who had been chosen bowed low, indicating her acceptance, and followed Vajix!krk back to the dais, taking a position in front of it as the G!at Councilor resumed her place among the other members of the Supreme Council.

They all looked expectantly toward Zeke. !Jng!xl spoke again, "Ezekiel Bones—who will be your champion?"

Aboard the *Ostrom*, Reelys had explained to them that the single combat challenge had arisen in order to let clans settle minor disputes without going to war. Such combat was normally between two !xaka! warriors. Clearly, Zeke could not fight the G!at soldier himself. But who would fight for him?

"Ezekiel Bones," !Jng!xl prompted, as the soldier Vajix!krk had chosen as G!at champion strutted back and forth in front of the dais. "You must choose your champion—or forfeit your claim to the slave."

Jackson knew some of the council members must be thinking Zeke would have to forfeit his claim—who, or what, besides one !xaka! warrior could take on another?

Yesterday, when they were discussing this contingency onboard the *Ostrom*, a similar, uncomfortable silence had come up.

Jackson had broken the silence then.

"Well," he'd said matter-of-factly, "I could do it."

They'd all stared at him like he'd lost his mind.

"Jackson," Reelys had been the first to speak. "Your suicide will not help matters appreciably."

"Yeah—are you crazy?" Marty added. "You're going to fight a !xaka! warrior to the death?"

"It wouldn't be the first time." Of course, the other had been a long time ago. He could barely remember the details of that battle—except that he'd won. But he was sure of one thing: "I'm a better fighter now."

Zeke had leaned against a wall in the main lab, just staring at him.

"I can do it," Jackson had said again. "Believe me."

"Choose your champion—or forfeit your claim to the slave, Ezekiel Bones," !Jng!xl repeated.

Zeke turned back to the dais.

"I choose Jackson Charles."

Jackson stepped forward to stand beside him. "I accept."

"A human?" Vajix!krk leaned over the dais, studying Jackson closely. She turned and spoke quietly with the Ghi!reeli councilor.

"They're probably wondering what kind of brain damage you have," Marty whispered.

Jackson glared at him.

Vajix!krk rose. "A moment, Councilor," she said to !Jng!xl. "Surely Ezekiel Bones cannot be serious—a human champion?"

Jackson answered for him.

"Dead serious," he said.

"I must remind you both—this fight *is* to the death," !Jng!xl said. "You are aware of this, Jackson Charles?"

Jackson nodded. "I am."

"This is unacceptable," Vajix!krk said. "The G!at will not be party to slaughter."

"Why do you hesitate?" the !van Councilor asked. "Surely you are not afraid of the human?"

Vajix!krk rose up and turned to face her accuser. "Do you accuse the G!at of cowardice, Councilor?"

All of a sudden, the Great Hall fell silent.

"What's going on?" Jackson whispered. "Why won't they fight me?"

Reelys moved alongside him. "The G!at at do not believe you are qualified to face the warrior they have chosen," s/he said.

"Not qualified?"

"You must forgive me, Jackson, but to even the most impartial eyes, a fight between you and the G!at champion would seem grossly unfair."

Jackson tried to look at the G!at warrior objectively. In addition to her superior size and strength, she had razor-sharp pincers, mandibles capable of shearing through metal, and was capable of spinning a webbing strong as rope and spraying a burning acid on her foes.

He looked down at himself.

"I'll grant it looks like an uneven match," he said.

Reelys continued. "To the G!at, most of whose soldiers are specially trained u!xani, it seems even more so. Under such circumstances, to the Councilor—and to many others—victory for their champion would make the G!at seem like little more than executioners."

Jackson frowned. "They wouldn't mind killing me—if they thought I had a chance at winning, is that right?"

"Exactly."

"Now I understand."

Jackson turned his attention back to the dais. The G!at champion caught his eye and made a hiss/click!ing noise. He had the feeling she wouldn't mind killing him, fair fight or not.

"All respect, Councilor—I did not mention the word 'cowardice.' I simply asked why you will not proceed with the challenge."

The Ghi!reeli Councilor broke in. "Ezekiel Bones—surely you do not expect your human can defeat a !xaka! warrior?"

Zeke smiled. "All respect, Councilor—but I do. Else I would not have offered challenge."

"The combat must proceed," the !van Councilor said.

"I am forced to agree," !Jng!xl said. "Challenge has been offered and accepted, champions have been chosen."

"No!" Vajix!krk said, staring angrily at Zeke.

"Then I move the G!at claim be set aside, and the human's honored," the !van Councilor said.

Many of the soldiers nearest the dais shifted position, and tightened their hold on their weapons. The great columns of soldiers behind them closed ranks.

Jackson didn't need to be an expert in !xaka!ian body language to know what that meant.

"Things are about to get pretty ugly here, Doc," Jackson said, stepping up alongside Zeke.

"I'm open to suggestions," Zeke said.

"I suggest we make a quiet exit, and stay away till things cool down."

Zeke shook his head. "It's not going to cool down—not even if we go away for good."

Reelys moved forward along Zeke's other side and said something to him.

Zeke smiled as he listened.

When Reelys was done talking, Zeke turned to Jackson and put a hand on his shoulder.

"Reelys has an idea," he said. He told him.

Jackson took a deep breath, and nodded.

"Councilors—I have a suggestion," Zeke declared, turning back to the dais. "If you feel my champion is not fit to face the G!at warrior, then test him—as you would test any other."

For a moment, the conversation stopped, and the Great Hall fell silent again.

Then it erupted for a second time.

"Impossible—"

"The human will never pass the first *!dza*—"

Over the cacophony, Jackson heard Marty talking to Zeke.

"I gotta hand it to you, Doc—you've upset more tradition here in the last hour than anybody else has in the last fifty years."

Zeke shrugged. "It was all Reelys's idea."

The hlidsjki's face fell slightly.

Jackson tapped Zeke on the shoulder. "What exactly do these tests involve?"

On the dais, !Jng!xl struggled to maintain some semblance of order.

"Councilors! Please—we have before us a motion to certify the human as a warrior."

"Accepted," Vajix!krk said. It was clear she had no further desire to prolong the debate.

"All respect—should not the question be put to the chamber?" the !seri Councilor asked.

"If the Councilor desires," Vajix!krk said. "I am leaving."

She swept down the dais to the floor of the Great Hall again, a column of soldiers trailing in her wake.

"The Diet is now in recess," !Jng!xl declared.

Soldiers broke ranks all around them, and the crowds in the galleries began to exit the Great Hall.

"Councilor—a moment!" Zeke called out to Vajix!krk. Vajix!krk turned.

"All respect—I would discuss this matter with you further, in private."

Vajix!krk nodded. "Very well—in private, and alone. All respect—but this matter does not concern Reelys."

"All respect, Councilor—it most certainly does," the shri began. "Kadak!xa was a colleague of mine—"

"It's all right," Zeke said. "Wait for me here."

"I don't see that we have anywhere else to go," Jackson pointed out.

"If you're not back in an hour, we'll send in the cavalry," Marty said.

"We *are* the cavalry," Zeke reminded him. He saw several members of the Supreme Council watching them closely.

"See if you can find out anything about Sylvie," he instructed, then turned and followed Vajix!krk out of the Great Hall.

Matters had not proceeded as planned.

That a human would invoke challenge. . . .

It was unthinkable. It must have been the shri.

No matter. The elements were all in place. But they would have to be watched carefully, lest the mixture bubble over too soon. The humans, in particular—their behavior could not be predicted. A wrong word at this stage, and war could conceivably erupt.

That would be inconvenient, though not disastrous.

As long as it was the right war.

Vajix!krk preceded Zeke down a long, straight hallway into a newer building—one of the towers he'd glimpsed before from outside, he presumed.

They emerged into a reception area. Directly in front of them sat a half-dozen !xaka!, busily working behind a series of video displays. Above their heads a huge image of a !xaka! claw, inlaid directly in the wall in gleaming silver, held a digging tool set in gold.

The one constant across the galaxy, Zeke thought. Bureaucracy in action.

As Vajix!krk entered, one of the !xaka! rose and bowed.

"Two messages, Councilor, and a further report on the damage to the workers' complex—"

"Not now." Vajix!krk brushed past, barely noticing the other. "I will be in conference." She moved down the hall, finally stopping before a door where two soldiers stood guard.

"My office," she told Zeke, waving him in behind her. One of the soldiers followed them in and remained by the door. "One moment, please."

Vajik!krk crossed to another video console built into the far wall, giving Zeke a chance to look the room over. He was impressed.

At first glance, he was tempted to compare this room to a painting he'd seen once of the Roman Imperial Palace at Constantinople. Opulence for the sheer sake of it.

The walls were coated with some kind of fabric—itself a luxury on Ahng—and brightly colored cushions lay strewn about the floor. Jewels of every size and conceivable shape were prominently displayed along shelves that ran the length of the room, with oddly shaped sculptures of metal interspersed among them. Scattered across the room were larger works carved directly from stone, and the walls were covered by a series of metal etchings.

Still, something other than mere opulence had been at work here—there was an underlying method to this madness. A method he recognized. As Vajik!krk turned back to face him, Zeke spoke.

"We share a common interest, I see. A fascination with the past."

Vajix!krk bowed low.

"Among the G!at, I am considered something of an archaeologist, though a more accurate translation of what I do would be 'collector.'"

"This is an impressive collection," Zeke said. He picked up a thin metal tube about two feet long and a few centimeters in diameter off one of the shelves.

"Ah—the !kan," Vajix!krk said. "A ceremonial weapon, used by the ancient priests of N'Gossa."

Zeke held the tube up and studied it. It was surprisingly light, and though it felt sturdy enough, he didn't see how it could be used as a weapon. He said as much to the Councilor.

"Watch," she said, taking it from him. She pressed a raised bump at the bottom of the tube—and two thin blades suddenly shot out from either side of the tube.

Vajix!krk spun the tube expertly in her hand, like a small propeller.

Zeke admitted it looked very much like a weapon now.

She pressed the blades down carefully and handed the !kan back to him. Zeke set it down and continued his examination of the Councilor's collection, turning to the etchings on the wall next.

The style of art used was more abstract than representational, though one of the scenes looked somehow familiar. . . .

"This looks like the Great Hall," Zeke said.

Vajix!krk indicated acknowledgement. "You are correct. A great deal of the objects in this room were recovered from our excavation of the ruins."

Zeke nodded. From what little he knew about !xaka!ian art, that time period seemed about right. Still, if he was going to look at relics recovered from the ancient city, there was one particular set of objects he was particularly interested in.

"What about the Scrolls?" Zeke asked. "Do you keep any of those here?"

Vajix!krk grew suddenly still, and silent. A moment passed, and Zeke felt the temperature in the room drop ten degrees. Finally the G!at Councilor spoke.

"Is that the real reason you came here, Ezekiel Bones? To look at the Scrolls?"

"No!" Zeke said, letting his anger show momentarily. "All respect—I'm here for Kadak!xa. That's all."

"Good—I am glad to hear you say that. The Scrolls are *our* property, *our* concern, and we will decide who looks at them. Is that understood?"

Zeke nodded, and decided not to force the issue. He did intend to examine the Scrolls, however, and the severity of the Councilor's reaction surprised and puzzled him.

Why was she so concerned about who looked at the Scrolls?

"Now, if you have something to discuss with me—"

"I do," he said.

Vajix!krk settled down on one of the many cushions lining the floor. Zeke followed suit, squatting down cross-legged directly opposite her.

"The G!at respect strength in all their dealings," Reelys had told him aboard the *Ostrom*. "You must never appear indecisive, or unable to back up your words with action. A moment of weakness, perceived or real, and they will simply take what they desire."

Zeke studied the G!at Councilor. Certainly she could take Kadak!xa from him, and he would be powerless to stop her. If Reelys hadn't discovered that archaic challenge rule, she would have done just that.

Vajix!krk took a small nugget from a ceramic bowl next to her, and offered it to Zeke.

"A delicacy," she said, "from the depths of our ocean. Please."

He nodded thankfully, took the nugget from her, popped it into his mouth. . . .

And nearly cracked a tooth.

Vajix!krk picked up another nugget from the bowl and popped it into her undermouth. Zeke took the opportunity to spit out the one she had given him and shove it into the pocket of his cold-suit.

"Councilor," he began. "I asked to see you because I feel the challenge is unnecessary."

"Unnecessary? Of course it is unnecessary. Cede your claim to the slave."

"That's not what I meant," Zeke said. "I am prepared to offer you a deal."

"A deal? What kind of a deal?"

He leaned forward intently.

"Let me buy Kadak!xa's contract from you."

"Buy her?" Vajix!krk said. She popped another nugget. "An intriguing thought—for the right price, it would be possible."

"Good," Zeke said.

She named a figure that would have rendered Zeke penniless.

He laughed, shook his head, and named another that would not have paid for the boots he was wearing.

Vajix!krk glared at him. "We have very different opinions of the slave's worth."

"Of course," Zeke said. "I suggest these negotiations may take some time."

"I must discuss your offer with others of my clan," Vajix!krk said.

"As I must discuss yours with my companions."

"Your shri, no doubt."

"No doubt."

"Very well." The Councilor shifted position on her cushion. "In the meantime, the testing of your champion must begin."

"Why?" Zeke asked, frowning. "Are the tests still necessary? Haven't we agreed that I will buy Kadak!xa's contract from you?"

"You invoked the challenge, Ezekiel Bones. You suggested the testing. I cannot stop the process until we reach agreement on a price for the slave—or it will seem to the other clans that we are backing down."

Zeke sighed and nodded, wondering how he could explain this to Jackson. "All right."

Vajix!krk offered him another nugget from the bowl. He shook his head.

"All respect, Ezekiel Bones—we would not find ourselves in this situation if the slave had not been foolish enough to come here."

Zeke did not expect that. Plain speaking from a !xaka!. Fair enough.

"All respect, Councilor—she was only foolish in believing the lies you told her."

The soldier by the door hiss/click!ed angrily. Vajix!krk lifted an arm, warning her back.

Zeke wondered if he'd spoken a little too plainly.

"You must explain that statement, Ezekiel Bones," Vajix!krk said, lifting herself off the cushion. "Or I shall be inclined to let my soldier explain hers to you."

Zeke looked at the soldier, who was still click!ing her claws together.

Never back down, Reelys had said.

"I simply meant what I said—if you hadn't changed that message, Kadak!xa would never have come here. All respect."

"What message? What are you talking about?"

Zeke studied the Councilor. Her anger seemed genuine.

"I am talking about the fact that the only reason Kadak!xa came to Ahng was to visit her father—who she thought was dying!"

"And you think we sent this message?"

"Yes," Zeke said. "I do."

"You must think we are fools." Vajix!krk rose and crossed to the communications panel again.

"*Councilor.*"

"!Zha!xir—how did we discover the escaped slave was returning to Ahng?"

"*Notification by an informant, Councilor.*"

"The name of this informant?"

"*V!xcl, Councilor—no clan affiliation.*"

"I see. Have this informant located and brought to me."

"*Yes, Councilor.*"

Vajix!krk closed the channel and turned to Zeke again. "You see? We used no false message to capture your slave."

"All respect—I see that *you* didn't," Zeke said, not entirely convinced of even that. "But perhaps another member of your clan did."

"Who among us would go to such trouble for a single escaped slave? Especially now—this incident is a distraction and an irritant at a time when we can least afford—" Vajix!krk broke off suddenly.

"Well, if you didn't send that message, who did?" Zeke asked.

Vajix!krk said nothing, but Zeke had a feeling she was trying to answer the same question.

"You must excuse me, Ezekiel Bones. I have other pressing matters to attend to."

She nodded to the soldier, who moved forward and stood by Zeke's side.

"Wait," Zeke said. He hadn't had a chance to ask about Sylvie yet. "All respect—I have another matter to discuss—"

"See one of the o!xer outside," Vajix!krk said.

The soldier gripped Zeke's arm with one of its claws—not hard enough to hurt, but hard enough to make him move with her toward the door.

"What about the tests?" Zeke called out. "And the negotiations?"

"The o!xer," Vajix!krk said. "Goodbye, Ezekiel Bones." The door closed.

In the hall, Zeke shrugged free of the soldier's grip.

"This way." The soldier indicated Zeke should precede her—in a way that made it clear it would be foolish to do anything else but that.

Significantly more puzzled than he had been before his meeting, he set off down the hall.

Jackson and Marty grew bored waiting for Zeke. Reelys, however, kept busy.

But then, once his'er identity became known, s/he had expected that.

All the members of the Supreme Council save Vajix!krk had remained in the Great Hall, and one by one, they approached him'er.

The !van Councilor was the first.

"I would be honored if you would dine with me this evening," she began, bowing low. "There will be many delicacies and many great personages assembled—and of course, we have matters of mutual interest to discuss—"

"Such as the talks on Sersic-4?"

Reelys did not enjoy the elaborate charades the !xaka! used to clothe their conversations in, and preferred to dispense with them whenever possible.

"Well—yes, but—"

"A moment," Reelys said. "I am willing to speak with you on that subject—but you understand that I am here as a friend of Ezekiel Bones, and not as a representative of my government?"

"Of course."

"Under those circumstances, I would be willing to listen to what you have to say. But I will make no attempt to hide this conversation from any of the other clans."

"But you will relay my thoughts to your superiors—"

"Colleagues," Reelys corrected. !Xaka! were often unable to comprehend how the shri conducted their affairs without a discernible decision-making hierarchy.

"—to your colleagues?"

"I will if they seem to me of value," Reelys said.

The !van Councilor clicked her mandibles several times before finally responding. "They are intrinsically of value," she said.

Reelys listened to her talk for five minutes, a steady stream of complaints about the G!at. She said nothing different from what her subordinates on Sersic-4 had said.

Nor did the Ghi!reeli Councilor—or the !seri—or the !xamini—or any of the others.

Perhaps it *had* been foolish to expect the !xaka! to be reasonable.

"Forgiveness—Ahnast Jhiilla?"

It was !Jng!xl.

"I prefer to be known as Reelys these days, Councilor."

"Reelys, then. If you have not grown tired of the subject, I would like to discuss with you the matter of the black hole transfer station."

Reelys drew his'er mantle up straighter.

"I have not grown bored of the subject, Councilor—with all due respect, I *have* grown bored with the recitation of complaints by your fellow Councilors."

!Jng!xl bowed slightly. "I have no complaints, Reelys. And truth to tell, I too grow bored with the complaints of my fellow Councilors at times."

"Then we have that much in common, at least. Tell me your thoughts."

"I have not been privy to all the talks, naturally—but my understanding is that there is clear sentiment for locating the transfer station closer to Ahng. It would profit a great many more clans."

"You are correct. It would profit a great many more clans were the station situated near here—including your own, I presume—but it would not profit the G!at. And the currently signed agreements call for the station to be built where they desire it. It seems to me that unless they can be persuaded otherwise, that is where the station will be built."

"Surely that is unjust."

"Perhaps—it depends on whose point of view one considers, does it not? The location was treaty-ratified by the Diet."

"A half-century ago—by a Diet subserviant to the interests of the G!at. Should a whole planet pay now for the injustices of the past?"

"Can you convince the G!at to change their position?"

"No," !Jng!xl said. "But perhaps you can."

"How would you suggest doing that?" Reelys asked.

!Jng!xl leaned closer. "You have the power."

"Break the treaty?" Reelys was astounded.

"I do not ask this idly. But I fear the Diet may rule against the G!at sometime this session, and petition the Galactic Worlds themselves to break the treaty."

"Would that not be the best possible solution?" Reelys asked.

"It would not. You do not understand, Reelys. The G!at will never accept an alteration of the treaty forced on them by the other clans. If that happens, they will go to war. I know it."

"Whereas if we broke the treaty—"

"They would demand compensation—but they would never attack you."

Reelys considered what !Jng!xl had told him'er.

"No. I cannot speak for my colleagues of course, but I feel confident their answer would be the same. If we broke this agreement, who could trust us on any other? The Galactic Worlds themselves are built on such contracts. More than any other race, we shri cannot break treaties when it suits our convenience."

"All respect, Reelys—then you are condemning my planet to war."

"I hope it will not come to that, Councilor."

!Jng!xl exhaled audibly. "As do I. Perhaps I am wrong."

"Perhaps," Reelys said. S/he was suddenly tired—the cumulative effect of all these draining conversations, coupled with the particularly weak lighting within the Great Hall.

!Jng!xl looked around. "Where is Sylvie Pharr? I was looking forward to talking with her again."

Jackson and Marty turned as one.

"You know Sylvie?"

!Jng!xl nodded. "We have become friends of a sort."

"We don't know where she is," Marty said. "When did you see her last?"

"Yesterday afternoon. I told her we had received word of your arrival. She seemed eager to see you all."

"Well?" Marty asked, spreading his arms. "Where is she?"

"I know of nothing which could have delayed her—unless, of course, she had further problems with the G!at—"

"Further problems?"

"An incident in one of our museums," !Jng!xl said. She told them what had happened to Sylvie and herself the day before.

"Let me ask you a question," Marty said. "Do you think the G!at imprisoned her?"

!Jng!xl thought a moment before answering. "It is hard to say. The Councilor can be difficult, but—I suspect something else must have happened to delay her."

Reelys agreed.

"I am sure she will find you shortly." !Jng!xl bowed. "I must take my leave of you. When Sylvie does return, please ask her to contact me."

She left—just as Zeke and another !xaka! rejoined them.

"What happened, Ezekiel?" Reelys asked. "How did the talks go?"

"All right—I think," Zeke said. "Did you find out anything about Sylvie?"

They told him of !Jng!xl's account. "We still haven't heard from her—I checked with Herb, too. And now he can't reach Ho!xa, either."

"That's odd," Zeke said. "I wonder where she is."

"It seems obvious to me where she is," Marty said angrily. "Somewhere else in the Keep. I think you were right before—the G!at kidnapped her just like they kidnapped Kadak!xa!"

Zeke shook his head. "The o!xer says she knows nothing about Sylvie," he nodded at the !xaka! who had accompanied him, "and I'm inclined to think Vajix!krk doesn't know where she is either. She also denied sending the message that brought Kadak!xa here in the first place." He relayed the substance and the tone of his conversation with the G!at Councilor.

"Oh come on, Zeke," Marty said. "Of course they're going to deny it. But who else would have sent the message?"

Zeke shook his head. "I don't know," he admitted.

"And tell me this," Marty replied. "If the G!at didn't arrest Sylvie—where is she now?"

The workers' complex was entirely devastated.

The soldiers combing the grounds did not expect to find anyone still alive. But they had orders—and besides, even though these were slaves' quarters, one never knew what trinket might show up.

!Dana, a recent u!xani addition to the G!at army, was burrowing through the wreckage in sub-level three when something caught her eye.

She scurried over heaps of fallen debris, and came to the small globe she had seen gleaming in the distance.

She picked it up and examined it closely. There was writing on one side—human writing. Three letters.

UCI.

She had been told to watch for those letters.

Setting the globe aside, she began to explore the rubble further.

Chapter Nine

"Now this," Marty said, feet firmly planted in the doorway, hands on hips, "is decadence."

Jackson gave him a little shove forward into their new quarters, then stopped at the threshold himself and set his gear down. He gave a long, low, appreciative whistle.

"You aren't kidding." He turned to Zeke, standing silently behind him. "How many of us do they think there are?" he whispered.

Before Zeke could respond, Reelys floated past them both, his'er eyestalks raised to scan the room, and uttered a single word. "Impressive."

Jackson and Zeke both nodded and followed him'er in, the click of their boot heels echoing off the hard stone floor.

Everywhere Zeke looked, the room was indeed impressive. Three walls and the ceiling above practically shone with patterns of inlaid white tiles, and the fourth wall was a series of bay windows, offering a spectacular view of the Keep outside. A bare minimum of sleek, stylish furniture was scattered about the room, and one entire corner was taken up by a videoscreen and a cabinet full of data solids (probably an entertainment library); Reelys had the cabinet open and was studying a half dozen or so that s/he held in his'er tentacles. There was even a comterminal next to it—although Zeke was certain it would be bugged.

The suite had clearly been designed with humans and species other than !xaka! in mind. The o!xer that had escorted them here could barely squeeze her bulk through the doorway.

"I hope you find this satisfactory," o!xer said. "The Councilor has entrusted me with the task of seeing that you are comfortable during your stay here, and I am anxious to see it fulfilled."

Zeke exchanged glances with his companions, and smiled. "I think we'll be fine here."

Despite her haste to get rid of him earlier, Vajix!krk had been true to her word. Not only had the o!xer arranged for this suite, but she had also scheduled the negotiations between Zeke and the G!at Councilors for the purchase of Kadak!xa.

"Your personal quarters are this way," the o!xer said.

"Personal quarters?" Jackson asked, peering around the huge room. "There's more?"

"Of course," the o!xer said. "Allow me to demonstrate." She walked over to one of three large, circular panels set into one of the walls, and pressed the center. The panel dilated to reveal a luxuriously appointed bedroom within.

"I have allocated yourself and the noble shri," she bowed to Reelys, "the two larger suites. Your warrior," she indicated Jackson, "will, unfortunately, have to share with your slave."

Marty's mouth dropped open.

"I'm not sharing with any slave," Jackson said.

The o!xer's mandibles clicked together rapidly. She crossed the room, and began bowing up and down rapidly in front of Zeke.

"Forgiveness, Ezekiel Bones—have I given offense?" she asked. "Perhaps you would prefer the slave be quartered with others of its caste, in the levels below, or—"

"No, no," Zeke said, winking at Jackson. "We'll figure something out. Thanks for your help."

Jackson laid a hand on Zeke's shoulder, and nodded. "It's not your fault about the slave. Maybe we'll have it sleep out here."

Marty was listening to their conversation in somewhat stunned silence, his eyes wide.

"I will take my leave of you, then," the o!xer said. "I am glad you are pleased."

She left, and the door slid shut behind her.

Zeke and Jackson burst out in laughter.

Marty walked over and planted a finger in Jackson's chest. "You know, that was not funny."

Jackson ignored him. "This place must be costing you a fortune, Doc," he said.

Zeke shook his head. "It's all free of charge."

"Free?"

"We're about to pay the G!at an awful lot of money for Kadak!xa," he said. "And if nothing else, the G!at know how to treat their business partners."

Reelys emerged from one of the private rooms, his'er tentacles fluttering. "Perhaps I shall have to revise my estimate of the !xaka! after all. This is truly a marvelous domicile—adjustable temperature controls, completely satisfactory lighting systems, hot and cold running water for you three to bathe in—we shall all be able to rest quite comfortably tonight."

Zeke ran a hand through his hair. A long, hot shower sounded pretty inviting right now, after being cooped up aboard the *Ostrom* for the last few weeks. He was looking forward to a good night's sleep as well—the next few days promised to be hectic.

"Hey, Doc, what about those tests?" Jackson asked. "When do we find out about them?"

Zeke shrugged. "The o!xer said we'd be contacted tonight or early tomorrow."

"Why the rush, anyway?" Marty asked. "Maybe Zeke and Reelys will settle the deal for Kadak!xa tomorrow, Sylvie'll show up, and we'll all go home."

"That'd be fine with me," Jackson said. "But just in case things don't work out that way, I want to be ready to fight."

"I would not be so eager, Jackson," Reelys said. "The u!xani are not as other !xaka!. My reading has shown me—"

The door buzzer sounded.

"Quick—answer that," Marty said. "Before Reelys gets going on another subject."

The shri exhaled in disgust and drew all its tentacles save the mouthstalk up into his'er central gas bag. "Rest assured, I shall not attempt any further enlightenment on your behalf, Marty," s/he said.

Jackson crossed to the door and ordered it to open.

A !xaka!, thinner than the o!xer had been, darker colored than any Jackson had seen before, stood outside the doorway.

"Ezekiel Bones?"

Jackson shook his head. "I'm Jackson Charles. That—" he nodded behind him at Zeke "—is Ezekiel Bones."

The !xaka! nodded. "I can speak to both of you. I am u!xani G!daeer, ordered by the Supreme Councilor to supervise your tests, Jackson Charles."

Jackson bowed. "Come in," he said.

The u!xani lifted her first segment as she entered, turning her head slowly to study the suite. "Luxurious," she said, then caught sight of the Keep outside. "Do you mind?" Without waiting for an answer, she crossed directly to the windows and stood by them a moment.

Jackson looked at Zeke, who just shrugged his shoulders.

"Forgive me," the !xaka! said, turning back to face them. "I have lived in the Keep all my life, serving the G!at Councilors—yet this is the highest level of the city I have ever been to." She said the words plainly, with no inflection, but even so, Jackson thought he could hear bitterness behind them.

Reelys jetted forward. "It is an extraordinary view," s/he acknowledged.

"You desire to become u!xani, Jackson Charles?" G!daeer said, deliberately turning her back on Reelys. That was a first—a !xaka! who didn't fall all over herself to get the shri's attention. Jackson filed that fact away for future reference.

He shook his head. "Not really. My interest is in completing the challenge. If I have to pass your tests in order to do that—"

The u!xani hissed. "These are not *my* tests, Jackson Charles. These are the tests !xaka! soldiers have taken for a thousand years, hoping to be counted among the elite warriors of our world. Many of the best soldiers never even have the opportunity to take them."

Jackson folded his arms and stared at the u!xani.

"I came here to tell you that the first test—the !*dza*, as we call them—will be tomorrow morning. Early. I will come here for you."

"Just tell me where to meet you," Jackson said. "I'll find it."

The u!xani bowed. "As you wish. There is a floatcar station at the lowest level of this tower. Be there at sunrise."

Jackson nodded. "Easy enough."

The u!xani paused a moment. "Of course, you will need your diving gear."

"Diving gear?"

"Indeed," the u!xani said. "The !dza all take place underwater."

"Wait a minute." Zeke, who had been silent up to this point, now spoke up. "The Councilor said nothing about making these tests underwater—"

"As I said before," the u!xani hissed. "No one is *making* these tests anything. They will proceed as they always have—underwater. We will not change a thousand years of tradition just because you have an underdeveloped set of gills."

Jackson glared.

"I will see you again tomorrow morning, Jackson Charles."

The door hissed shut behind her.

"Extraordinarily unfriendly, even for a !xaka!," Reelys declared.

"They don't seem pleased by the thought of a human joining their ranks," Zeke said.

"I'm not too excited by it either, to tell you the truth."

"I'm gonna take a shower, Jackson," Marty called out, heading for their room. "Unless you want one first."

"No, I don't think I'm going to take one at all," Jackson replied, sitting down heavily in a chair. "I have the feeling I'm going to get wet enough in the next few days to last me a lifetime."

Dawn on Ahng came suddenly, harsh as the blinding flare of a magnesium burst. Thanks to the lack of cloud cover and the thinness of the planet's atmosphere, there was no gradual sunrise, as on Earth. Within seconds after the sun first appeared over the horizon, it was too brilliant to stare at directly.

Beneath the ice it was another story altogether.

The sun's blinding rays were filtered and softened, first by their passage through layers of ice, then by the fresh-water seas themselves.

So what Jackson Charles saw the next morning, as he began preparations for the first of his tests, was an underwater world of blues and greens, of hazy, indistinct geologic formations lit by that filtered sun and a few artificial lights brought by the u!xani and her assistants who would supervise him.

He'd actually been up for hours already, having made the journey by shuttle out to the *Ostrom* and back for the depthsuits he and Marty were now wearing. That was the only pleasant thing that had happened to him on the whole trip so far—the fact that Marty had insisted on accompanying him for the tests.

Zeke had outfitted the *Ostrom* and its labs for every possible contingency, or they might have had to delay these tests for several days searching for underwater gear. But there were a lot of water worlds in the galaxy, and Zeke had counted on their visiting at least one of them, so they had state-of-the-art diving suits—thin, flexible, and equipped with two-way radios.

Jackson still felt stiff in the suit, however—especially when contrasted with the !xaka!, who moved naturally and gracefully through the water, their colorful gill plumes fully raised and spread behind them. It was certainly going to be a lot harder for him to pass any kind of physical test down here.

As several of the u!xani finished setting up the artificial lights (brought solely for his benefit, at Zeke's insistence—!xaka! vision, though shockingly limited above water, was superbly precise beneath it), G!daeer bent at the middle and, using her rear segments like a tail, kicked forward. A split second later, she glided smoothly alongside him.

She had been outfitted with a vocoder in order that Jackson could understand her underwater. He, in turn, had modified the thin, flex-mesh depth suit from the *Ostrom* with an external speaker—and an internal comm channel so he and Marty could communicate privately. Their suits also had a five-hour oxygen supply—more than enough time to take the test, G!daeer had assured him.

He certainly hoped so.

"What are they going to do with those poles?" a voice echoed in his ear.

He turned to Marty, treading water next to him, and shrugged. "We'll find out soon enough." He had to suppress an urge to laugh again; a hlidjski in a depth-suit was not one of the world's more graceful creatures, though Jackson had to give him an "A" for effort.

"Many of the trials a !xaka! must undergo have no analogue for humans," G!daeer began, "as they lack the internal weapons capacity of the !xaka!."

"A fancy way of saying you can't spin webs or spray acid, like them," Marty's voice echoed in his ear.

"Nonetheless, we have agreed on three tests which will roughly translate. This is the first. The !dza yeni—the trial of strength."

Marty pointed now, and Jackson saw two of the u!xani each grab one pole, and embed them firmly in the ocean floor, about three meters apart.

"You must move in between them," the u!xani stated.

Jackson did as he was told, swimming forward gracefully and positioning himself at a point roughly midway between the two poles.

G!daeer made a loud, clicking noise—and the two who had carried the poles began to quickly spin webbing thick as rope from one of their middle segments. They used it to fasten Jackson's limbs securely between the two poles, in a spreadeagle position. He tested the webbing. It was like steel.

"Now what?" Jackson asked.

"Now break your bonds," she said, swimming in front of him. "Now escape."

In the privacy of his'er quarters, Reelys took the extraordinary step of establishing instantaneous direct contact with the shri negotiators on Sersic-4 half a galaxy away.

It was an ability that the shri used rarely, and always with great reluctance. For although the ability was innate, it was also somewhat dangerous (Reelys suspected it had something to do with the manipulation of the "superspace" through which they communicated), and had often resulted in inexplicable, explosive releases of destructive energy.

The shri had never revealed this ability to the other civilized races in the galaxy, partly out of fear that others would discover how to manipulate the energies involved and use them for less scrupulous purposes, and partly because it enabled them to maintain certain advantages they had no interest in ceding, especially to races as immature as the !xaka!.

"*Soshera,*" Reelys flashed. "*I am glad to speak with you.*"

"*As I you, Ahnast, although I wish I had happier news. The G!at delegates here have walked out on negotiations. I do not think they will return.*"

"*The situation here bears remarkable similarity to yours, then.*" S/he told Soshera about the dispute that had arisen as a result of the rival claims to Kadak!xa's services, and the G!at's growing isolation from the other clans as a result of that dispute.

"*Have you been able to speak with the clan leaders?*" Soshera asked.

"*Several have contacted me regarding the talks, openly expressing the fear that if we do not force the G!at to accept the new location for the transfer station, clan war is inevitable.*"

Soshera was silent a moment. "*I believe they are correct,*" s/he finally indicated. "*The coming clan war is inevitable.*"

"*Agreed,*" Reelys flashed. "*But it must spread no further.*"

Soshera acknowledged his'er understanding. "*I will contact Griynsh, then—for barring unforeseen occurrences, I expect all !xaka! delegates will withdraw and return to Ahng within the next few days.*"

"*I may not be able to contact you again before our business here is concluded. But my thoughts will remain with you.*"

"*As mine will remain with you, Ahnast. Soshera out.*"

Reelys broke contact successfully, and floated in the darkness of his'er room, thinking, for a time.

He needed a miracle, Jackson decided. Nothing short of that was going to break these bonds.

"Four hours," Marty said over the comm link. "What are you thinking?"

"That this was a really bad idea," Jackson said. He tugged at the webbing that bound his left wrist angrily, but it didn't give an inch. He'd tried everything—pulling with all his might to one side, quickly alternating pulling between sides, scraping the webbing against the steel poles, and just plain thrashing. None of it had worked.

G!daeer swam in front of him again.

"Do you wish to concede failure?"

"No," Jackson said, biting his lip hard. He wasn't going to give up until he absolutely had to.

"You have not broken even one strand of the webbing," she said.

"I'm counting on a miracle," he said.

The u!xani's eyes glittered. "U!xani do not count on miracles—only on themselves."

"I hate to say this," Marty began, "but we're running low on air."

"I'm not quitting," Jackson said.

Just then, he felt the poles shift slightly.

"What the—"

Now they began shaking violently. The other u!xani were clicking at each other furiously.

"It's an earthquake!" Marty said, twisting his body around.

A shock wave slapped at Jackson, stretching the webbing, then moved past, hitting Marty. It sent him spinning off into the dark ocean, and he was quickly lost from sight.

"Marty!"

Jackson twisted futilely. But the ground beneath him shook again—and one of the poles snapped. His right arm and leg were suddenly free to move.

"Find him!" he yelled to one of the u!xani, pointing in the direction where Marty had disappeared. Using the webbing still stuck to his right arm, he drew half of the snapped pole to him, and began using the edge where it had broken to saw through the webbing.

By the time he had released himself, the u!xani had returned with Marty in tow, and the earth tremors had stopped.

"I'm free," Jackson said.

"You did not break the bonds," G!daeer stated.

"But I escaped," Jackson said, holding up a strand of webbing that floated by in the water. "My miracle came through."

The other two u!xani were looking at Jackson strangely. Maybe he was just imagining it, but he thought he saw a trace of awe in their eyes.

"Very well—you have passed the first !dza," G!daeer said grudgingly. "Albeit in a most unusual manner."

Marty swam up next to him, and helped slide the last piece of webbing off his ankle.

"I think this is how religions get started," he said over the comm link. "Rumors of your divinely inspired feat are going to spread like wildfire."

Jackson shook his head. He didn't feel too divine right now. Just incredibly lucky.

Zeke and Reelys had just started negotiations when the tremor struck. The G!at tower was not damaged at all, but nonetheless, a recess was immediately called, which suited Zeke just fine.

Things were not going well.

The G!at had modified their initial, exorbitant demands somewhat, but had now expressed their desire to tie this deal to a new one with the Bones Energy Corporation, wherein their subsidiaries would become exclusive distributors in this region for BEC deuterium. Deuterium, essential to the safe operation of the matter/antimatter space drive, was one of the more valuable commodities in the galaxy.

Zeke had spent an hour trying to explain to them that just because his name was Bones, he could not unilaterally conclude deals for that multi-trillion dollar organization.

"Not to mention the fact that the Board of Directors would have a fit if I even suggested such a thing," he told Reelys. They were standing in an antechamber in the G!at tower.

"Perhaps that is how we need to proceed," Reelys said, "impress upon them that you are, in fact, an employee as well and that you have only limited company resources, as well as your personal assets, to draw upon."

"That's what I've been trying to do for the last hour!" Zeke said, more sharply than he'd intended. He'd been on edge the whole day—they'd still had no word from or about Sylvie, and Jackson and Marty had yet to return from the first test.

From the other end of the corridor, two warriors approached. As they drew closer and saw Reelys, they bowed their heads lower, making sure to give the shri a wide berth.

"Perhaps you will allow me to try," Reelys suggested. "I believe I may have more success, given that the G!at are predisposed to hear what I say as coming from a superior."

Zeke nodded.

He could see why Marty sometimes felt Reelys was a bit annoying.

"Shall we return to the chamber?" Reelys asked.

"Ezekiel Bones!"

He turned, and saw Vajix!krk coming down the hall to them, two soldiers trailing in her wake.

"I hope the tremors did not disturb you. An unfortunate fact of life here, such things."

"You have these a lot?"

"They come and go in cycles—and we appear to be in the middle of one such cycle now. My apologies."

Zeke nodded.

"My u!xani have yet to find the informant we discussed yesterday—the one who told us the slave was coming—but we will," the Councilor stated, emphasizing her last words with several clicks from the !xaka!ian language. "I have, however, just received some unfortunate news of your reporter friend."

Zeke's stomach turned over.

"Early yesterday, there was another, much more severe earth tremor in the workers' complex outside the Keep, where the slave's brother lived. We have reason to believe that your reporter friend, Sylvie Pharr, was killed in that earth tremor," Vajix!krk said. She motioned one of the u!xani behind her forward. The u!xani handed her a small, clear globe, about the size of a softball.

"This was recovered from the rubble by one of the u!xani," Vajix!krk said, handing the globe to Zeke.

He turned it over in his hands, his mind reeling.

It was one of Sylvie's holocams. She wouldn't have let anything happen to it—if she could prevent it.

He looked up at the G!at Councilor.

"I am sorry, Ezekiel Bones. The complex was completely destroyed," she said. "No survivors were found."

Chapter Ten

Cold metal pressing against her cheek, along the length of her body. A sharp pain at the back of her head, a relentless pounding inside her skull—those were her first sensations. Then a dull throbbing in her left ankle— had she broken something there?—and dried blood on her cheek and in her hair and on her scalp. She must have cracked her head pretty hard—

The earthquake. The G!at soldiers, and Ho!xa. Dead, all of them.

Her eyes flickered open, and she groaned softly.

Sylvie Pharr was alive.

She was lying on the floor of a small room, identical to the cell she had visited Kadak!xa in. Four featureless walls, the circular outlines of a door opening in one of them, an ambient light source somewhere in the ceiling—and nothing else.

Someone must have brought her here—but who? Where was she? Where were they? Where was Zeke?

She had to get up, get some answers. She pushed her-self up one elbow.

The effort almost cost her what little food was left in her stomach, and sent her head spinning worse than ever.

Sylvie lay down again and shut her eyes. The floor felt cool and soothing against her forehead—did she have a fever? No, that was crazy—you couldn't get a fever from an earthquake.

Only a minute, she told herself. *Only rest a minute.*

She passed again into oblivion.

Sylvie had no way of knowing it, but it was now morning of the third day since the earthquake that had knocked her unconscious, and Jackson Charles was preparing for the second test that would certify him as u!xani.

There were more !xaka! present this time—o!xer and u!xani from several clans—drawn, he guessed, by news of the "miracle" that had enabled him to pass the first test at all. He hoped he wouldn't let them down.

G!daeer swam up next to him.

"Are you prepared for the second !dza?"

Jackson held up his hand. "Give me a minute." He turned to Marty, who had been uncharacteristically silent that morning, and spoke to him over the depth-suit radio. "What's bugging you?"

"I'm worried about Zeke," Marty said glumly. "The news about Sylvie hit him pretty hard."

"It hit us all pretty hard," Jackson said. "But he'll get over it." They had all seen death before—maybe not this close up, not for a while, but it happened. The trick was to put it behind you, to get on with living. Survival was the name of the game.

"You're pretty cool about the whole thing, aren't you?"

Jackson gritted his teeth angrily.

"Look, Marty—what do you want me to do? Fall apart because Sylvie's dead? That's not going to help anything. She's gone—and there's nothing any of us can do about it."

Marty stared at him. Even through the facemask of his depth-suit, the stony look on his face was easy to see.

"Right. Forget I said anything." He turned and began swimming away in the other direction.

"Marty—wait!" With one powerful kick of his legs, Jackson drew up alongside him. "Where are you going?"

"Back to the city," the hlidjski's voice came back. "To maybe fall apart a little. You don't need me here."

Jackson watched as he swam out of sight.

"Great," Jackson said. "Just great."

"Where is your companion going?" G!daeer asked. "He will miss the test."

"Back to the city," Jackson repeated.

"Ah." She waved two of the u!xani forward. "They will accompany him."

"That won't be necessary," Jackson said. He had visions of Marty starting a minor war if he found two !xaka! acting as nursemaids for him. "He can find his own way."

"As you wish." She waved the others back into formation.

"All right," Jackson said, trying to sound more confident than he felt. "I'm ready for the next test."

G!daeer uttered a series of clicks, and the u!xani swam forward, and formed a circle around him. There were perhaps a dozen altogether.

From harnesses strapped to their bodies, they each withdrew a small hand-weapon, and aimed at Jackson.

"The !dza meni—the trial of speed and stamina," G!daeer said.

The door to Sylvie's cabin slid open.

Zeke walked in, carrying Sylvie's damaged holocam in one hand. He threw it on her bed.

"Close. Private." He wanted to be alone in here awhile.

The cabin was exactly as Sylvie must have left it to visit Ahng with Kadak!xa and Marty. She'd had the *Ostrom* shape the memory plastic of the room into a desk and chair, a bed, some shelving—nothing elaborate, certainly nothing compared to what the system was capable of, just a simple area for her to work and sleep in. Articles of clothing, data solids, some sheets of printout were still scattered about the room. She must have told the shipboard computer to leave her things alone, or the autobots would've come in and cleaned up. A single, deep storage shelf ran across the room atop the bed. On it were the rest of Sylvie's bags. Zeke would bet money that everything tangible she'd owned in the world was in this room.

She'd taken it all with her when she left the Bones estate in Africa, planning to follow the story that had brought her here wherever it went—just like she'd followed so many others over the years Zeke had known her. He hadn't even wanted her to come this far, to Ahng. The short time they'd had together in Africa had been the first they hadn't been on some kind of assignment. Zeke had enjoyed that time a lot. He wanted more of it.

Sylvie wanted to leave.

Zeke had been angry. They had fought.

And now she was dead.

He sat down on her bed. What would happen to everything here, to the rest of her assets—if she had any? Sylvie Pharr had been a very private person—he was only beginning to realize just how private. He'd really never known very much about her other than the surface details; she was passionate about her work, and about very little else. She had no close friends that he knew about, and after her parents had died, she hadn't stayed in touch with any of her relatives. Maybe she left instructions with her superiors at UCI on the disposition of her "estate"—he'd check when they got back to Earth.

There was a small box on a shelf running next to the bed. He opened it.

Inside was a small collection of jewelry—and the jhirba stone he'd given Sylvie a few years ago. The green jewel sparkled in his hand—brighter than any diamond, greener than any emerald, yet of little value beyond its beauty. The floors of Nicari's oceans were covered with stones just like this one, and after an expedition there, he'd brought back several of them for his friends.

It surprised and pleased him and made him sad, all at the same time, that Sylvie had kept hers so close.

He picked up the badly damaged holocam from the bed next to him. The data solid was still inside. He wondered what was on it.

"Herb."

"Here, Zeke."

"Play this for me," he said, inserting the solid into a slot in the cabin wall. He swung the comscreen around in front of him, and leaned back against the wall to watch. There was a soft whirr as the computer read the solid's contents.

"Problem, Zeke. The solid is badly damaged—as is most of the data on it."

Zeke frowned. "Well, that's not too surprising—these things just went through an earthquake. Map it onto another—"

"Won't help—the damage here isn't physical. Somebody zapped this solid with a grade-A electromagnetic field. For the most part, all that's left on this is noise. Some of the sectors don't seem to have been damaged, but they may not hold any data."

"Show me the undamaged sectors," Zeke ordered.

"Right." A few seconds pause. "This is the first."

An image flickered onto the comscreen next to him.

The house in Africa, Mahsi standing in front of it, showing Jackson how to clean and dress a gazelle. Then Sylvie, walking by in front—

"Enough," Zeke said. "Show me the next one."

A cave—somewhere. Sylvie's carrysack in the corner—

Then the screen went white. Noise.

"That's all there is to that one," Herb said. "Next sector."

Ground. Someone laughing. Sylvie. "No, Ho!xa. Aim the scanner over my shoulder—"

"Next."

A long, low display case, in the middle of a large, empty room. No—not empty. Voices—a !xaka!, and human.

"What do they say?"

Sylvie. Where was this?

She moved into the picture as the holocam tracked closer to the display case—he realized this must be the museum !Jng!xl had talked about meeting Sylvie in.

The display case. A series of metal tablets, inscribed with hieroglyphs—

"Good God," Zeke said. He sat up straight on the cabin bed, and felt a chill run down his spine. "Those are the Scrolls of N'Gossa."

He watched as the encounter in the museum he had been told about unfolded, till one of the G!at soldiers pulled out a hand-weapon, took aim directly at him, it seemed, and the screen went white again.

"You want the next sector?" Herb asked.

"No," Zeke said thoughtfully. "Run that one again. And make a copy of it."

"Freeze that image," he ordered when the tablets appeared on-screen. He stared at the objects archaeologists across the galaxy had dreamed of seeing, had written about for the last century.

The so-called "Scrolls of N'Gossa" were two thousand years old—on Earth, while these were being written, Attila the Hun was terrorizing Asia, and Rome was falling to the Vandals. The Dark Ages were about to descend over Europe, and Buddhism to begin its long, slow procession across China.

While on Ahng, the priests of ancient N'Gossa—from whom the G!at had descended—were guiding the !xaka! rise to civilization. What else had been happening on the planet? Why were the G!at rulers so secretive, so possessive of the Scrolls?

Did it have anything to do with what had happened to Sylvie?

This might be his only chance—the only chance for anyone—to find out.

"Herb, I want you to print out a hardcopy of these images, the best resolution you can get. No, wait—" he leaned forward and pulled the data solid out of the wall slot.

"Let's do this in the main lab."

He rose, and took a long, last look around Sylvie's cabin. He felt he still had unfinished business here—but his final goodbyes would have to wait now. He had work to do.

"And Herb—let's clean this place up."

"Right, Zeke."

The door shut behind him.

Jackson, treading water, turned slowly, taking in the circle of warriors that surrounded him.

"Each of the warriors holds a small hand-laser. They will fire one at a time, in a pre-arranged random sequence," G!daeer said.

"What do I do?" Jackson asked. If the first test had been impossible, this one seemed almost childish, like some schoolyard game.

"Simply dodge their fire—while remaining within the circle."

"Wait a minute—how am I supposed to—"

She explained that the warriors would each give a warning click before they fired.

"Demonstrate," she said.

A click!ing sound came from just behind him. He turned.

Just as a thin white beam lanced out and struck him on the arm.

"Ow," he said, swinging his arm up and out of the beam's path. Where the laser had struck him, the depth-suit next to his skin was burning hot. A second more of contact, and he would have been burned.

Talk about being on the hot seat. . . .

"The lasers are of course on their lowest settings. You are allowed three hits before you fail. The test will end when all of the warriors have fired twice." G!daeer clapped the claws of her third-segment legs together, a sharp sound that echoed through the water.

"Begin," she called out.

Jackson swiveled his head slowly, taking in the expressionless stares of the warriors who encircled him.

He recalled Zeke noticing how G!daeer hadn't been thrilled at the thought of him becoming u!xani, and suddenly wondered—how far would these !xaka! go to prevent a human from joining their "exalted" ranks?

There was another click behind him.

Jackson didn't bother trying to turn and identify which warrior was going to fire. The split second he heard the click, he threw himself violently to one side.

The laser burst caught him on the ankle, held there for a second. He screamed in agony.

He knew, without looking, that there were now second, maybe even third degree burns on his leg where the beam had struck.

Another click came, this one from off to his right.

He tried to throw himself back. The burst caught him squarely in the chest. It was like being splattered with hot coals. He gasped in pain, and used his legs to kick up and away.

"You cannot leave the circle, Jackson Charles," G!daeer called out, floating just beyond the ring of warriors. "You may of course call off the tests at any time."

He could swear he heard pleasure in her voice.

"Thanks," Jackson panted, "but I'm not ready to quit just yet." But he couldn't possibly handle this level of pain for too much longer. His ankle and chest both felt like they were on fire, and his heart was going full-tilt, pumping adrenaline and endomorphins into his system. No wonder they call this a test of speed and stamina, he thought. You couldn't dodge around like this unless you were in absolutely top condition.

He floated back down into the circle, turning slowly, using his arms to propel himself, studying each warrior as they swung past him, waiting for the next click, the next shot. They certainly were taking their time, making him sweat—probably enjoying this an awful lot, especially the obvious pain he was in.

He had a sudden, frightening thought.

What if the warriors were no longer using the lowest settings on their weapons?

If that were true, he'd better come up with some kind of strategy—and fast, or he wouldn't just fail the test. He might not make it out of here alive.

Perhaps if he could discern the pattern they were firing in . . . or a telltale move they made before they fired. . . .

Using the servo that had replaced his left eye, he scanned the entire width of the spectrum—and as he spun, he caught a flash of red at the tip of one of the warrior's hand-weapons.

A split second later, that same warrior click!ed and fired.

Jackson dodged easily.

He had his advantage. That dull red color—it must be the start of the firing sequence for the hand-lasers. To the !xaka!, that part of the spectrum was next to invisible—but to his augmented vision, it stood out like a beacon.

And that dull warning glow told him something else.

The u!xani were cheating. They were starting the firing sequence before click!ing to warn him of it.

He saw the tip of another warrior's weapon glow.

With a powerful scissors kick, Jackson propelled himself to one side.

The warrior click!ed once, and fired. The beam of light lanced through the spot where he had been.

Maybe luck—and whatever gods there were—really were on his side.

The test lasted another quarter-hour.

The u!xani never touched him again.

"It's me, Herb. Open up."

The ship's computer analyzed his voiceprint and retinal pattern, compared them with those of personnel authorized to enter the ship, found a match, and cycled the airlock.

Marty Szigmond trudged down the *Ostrom*'s corridors, feeling a little tired, a little foolish, and a lot useless.

Muscles he never knew he had ached from the swimming he'd done the last couple of days—especially the swimming he'd had to do to get from the test site back to the Keep.

Zeke hadn't been in the suite of rooms the G!at had given them. He hadn't been anywhere. Reelys barely had time to say that s/he hadn't seen Zeke all day before being called back into negotiations. The o!xer in the G!at tower wouldn't let him onto the higher-level floors to talk to the Councilor, and the workers near their suite of rooms hadn't seen him all day. So much for trying to lift someone else's spirits.

So much for trying to do anything at all.

It had been stupid of him to lose his head back at the test site. Jackson had more than enough to worry about without taking on the burden of Zeke's problems, as did everyone else, it seemed, except him. These last few days, he had really begun to feel like the proverbial fifth wheel around here—there was literally nothing for him to do. On most of the *Ostrom*'s normal expeditions, he was both mission planner and geologist, but this wasn't a normal expedition.

He'd decided to just leave them alone so they could all get their work done.

He hadn't come to the *Ostrom* to just sit around and mope, though—that, after all, was what he had been going to chastise Zeke for. He was here to do something useful— to finish cataloging the records from their last mission.

The door to the main lab slid open at his approach.

Zeke was sitting at a long low table across the room, a series of photos spread out before him, a mug of tea within easy reach. He didn't even look up, though Marty knew he'd heard him enter. And even before he spoke, Marty knew he wouldn't have to worry about not being busy anymore.

Zeke was working on something.

"You must have read my mind—I was just about to call you. Come here," Zeke said, motioning him over without looking up from the table. "I want you to take a look at these."

Chapter Eleven

It took them the next thirty-six hours to discover what the G!at were hiding.

Zeke had Herb access all the references he had on file concerning the discovery of the Scrolls. A century ago, it had been the biggest, most sensational news story in the galaxy. He had known that. But he hadn't known that the stories of the find that had blanketed the holovision channels had to concern themselves with rumors, and secondhand reports: not a single human journalist had been admitted to the ruins, not a single image of the site released. Of the partially corroded metal tablets the more sensationalist news agencies immediately dubbed "the Scrolls of N'Gossa," just as little was known. What meager scraps of information had been released, Zeke went on to tell Marty, related that the G!at workers had come upon the ruins while constructing the massive shuttle station just off N'Gossa. The Scrolls themselves had been found, relatively undamaged, just a few weeks later.

At first, the G!at had been openly boastful: Here at last was solid evidence of the fabled N'Gossa, as well as confirmation of their claims that they were the true descendants of that lost civilization. The planet's greatest scientists and all its clan leaders were invited to tour the ruins (one of the only firsthand reports of the site came years later from a deposed Councilor), and there was even talk of allowing aliens to visit the site.

And then suddenly, all that had changed. The second-hand rumors reaching human news agencies became third and fourthhand. A shri delegation, near to obtaining permission to copy the tablets for the Galactic Museum on Griynsh, was turned down flat, and asked to leave. All non-G!at scientists working at the site were expelled.

The news agencies reported that the G!at actions stemmed from increasing tension among the clans, increasing difficulties working together. And with each passing day, less and less information was released—until, finally, the dig was closed, and the Scrolls relegated to vaults deep within the Keep.

Several years later, the translations were released. The G!at *!x'kuta*—"the principles of order"—in particular made quite a splash, confirming as it did the G!at preeminence in planetary affairs.

Now, looking over the history of the Scrolls, their discovery and decipherment, Zeke grew suspicious. Marty shared those sentiments.

"Hell, Zeke, it doesn't take a Ph.D. to smell a rat there," he said.

That first night, using the translations that !Jng!xl had displayed for Sylvie, they tried to duplicate the G!at scientists' research, and establish a rough lexicon of all the hieroglyphs used by the ancient priests of N'Gossa. At the same time, they put Herb to work blowing up, enhancing, and refining the images of the rest of the tablets so they'd have the most legible hard copies possible to work from.

Herb came up with some wonderful prints.

Zeke and Marty came up with nothing.

They worked all through the next day without a break, never leaving the lab. Early that evening, Marty fell asleep at his desk.

Zeke let him rest. He put on another pot of tea and started over.

By morning, he'd found the problem.

It him him as he was studying the inscriptions on the !x'kuta. No matter how many contextual differences of meaning he was willing to allow for each glpyh, how many grammatical rules he was willing to establish and then stretch, he could come up with nothing resembling the G!at translation. He and Marty had easily been able to follow their work on the smaller ones, but here. . . .

It was like he was trying to decipher two different scripts, written in the same symbols.

He sat up straight in his chair, and exhaled softly.

"By God," he whispered. "It's Evans and Linear B, all over again."

There *were* two different languages in the tablets—and the G!at had successfully translated only one of them.

The smaller tablets—the lists of transactions, inventories, etcetera, the G!at had correctly interpreted. In fact, the language used in those tablets was a clear ancestor of the present-day G!at language.

But the language used on the larger tablet—the !x'kuta— was another story entirely. As far as he could tell, the G!at had simply invented their so-called "principles of order"— the !x'kuta may have been written with the same symbols as the other tablets, but they didn't mean the same thing.

No wonder Vajix!krk had been so suspicious when he'd asked about the Scrolls.

The other clans, who had ceded the G!at dominance in !xaka! affairs based in large part on these "principles of order," would find this news very interesting. Especially now, in light of the G!at's continued refusal to relocate the black hole transfer station.

He shook Marty awake.

"Huh?" Marty yawned, and cracked his eyes open. "Oh, it's you, Doc. Listen, we really ought to get a bed in here," he said. He shut his eyes and slumped back over the table.

Zeke shook him awake again.

Marty looked at Zeke irritably, then at the clock on the wall.

"I hope you have a damn good reason for getting me up. I missed getting my eight hours by a wide margin." He squinted up at Zeke. "You look like you haven't been getting your eight hours either."

"I haven't," Zeke said. "But let me tell you why."

By the time he was through talking, Marty was wide awake, and helping himself to a cup of tea.

Across the many worlds of the !xaka! empire, business had come to a screeching halt.

The information was evident in the unfolding display screens: The stalemate on Sersic-4 and the resulting increase in tension between the major !xaka! clans was the primary cause.

Trade among the colony worlds must resume soon, or their economies would begin to collapse. Yet an informant had just given word that the clans planned to recall their delegates from the conference within the next few days.

The time for talking, for easing those tensions, it seemed, was past. The time for war would soon be upon them.

Excellent.

Under the leadership of the !van, the majority of the clans would side against the G!at. The war would begin among the colony worlds, of course, but could easily spread to Ahng. Current projections indicated that the !van alliance would most likely emerge victorious, although significantly weakened.

Leaving the field clear for new leaders, who could shape the fragile balance of power between clans to their desires.

The onset of this war, then, must be encouraged—by all possible means.

There was a soft buzzer, and the sound of a door dilating open.

A hand waved over the controller circuit, clearing the display screens and their multitude of projections.

"Forgive the interruption, Councilor," the o!xer said, bowing. "Ezekiel Bones and a companion are here and wish to speak with you."

"Show them in, by all means."

!Jng!xl rose and prepared to greet her guests.

Unreasonable, but not impossible.

That was Reelys's impression of the G!at negotiators. After two days of talks, s/he felt they were at last close to agreeing on a price for Kadak!xa. Matters had been helped by Jackson's performance on the tests so far—his seemingly miraculous successes against what had been reported to Reelys as "a stacked deck" were being taken as the stuff of miracles by many of the lower-caste, less educated u!xani, and the G!at had grown anxious to close the deal before his reputation grew any larger.

"Then we are agreed," the primary G!at negotiator stated. This negotiator was male—one of the few in any position of prominence Reelys had come across. His first-segment hands were constantly in motion. He used them to punctuate all his statements, which only gave them an exaggerated effect Reelys found comical. The male also had a tendency toward bluster, no doubt an attempt to compensate for his diminutive stature. Vajix!krk, who was even now sitting in on these negotiations, was using him as a stalking horse, allowing him to present the more extreme positions. If those positions were not well received, she would then break in with more moderate compromises.

"Ezekiel Bones shall present the G!at subsidiary to the BEC as the new exclusive distributors for deuterium in this sector—"

"That is *not* what we have agreed to," Reelys answered, modulating his'er voice to make it sharper, harsher. S/he was annoyed at the male's constant attempts to reword his'er statements just enough to change their meaning, a foolish and potentially dangerous tendency s/he had noted among human lawyers as well. "Ezekiel Bones has promised to suggest the G!at subsidiary as new distributors at the next BEC Board of Directors meeting, but he cannot promise which way the Board will then decide."

"Surely, we are then entitled to some sort of compensation if the Board decides against us," the male said. "I would think—"

"We have been over this ground before," Reelys stated. "We feel the price we are prepared to pay is sufficient—"

S/he stopped in mid-sentence at a sudden clamor behind him'er.

Ezekiel Bones entered the room, dressed in the black and silver uniform he wore while engaged in scientific research. It was the first Reelys had seen of him in two days, and he looked as if he hadn't rested for a minute.

The in!chi Councilor, !Jng!xl, and Marty Szigmond entered directly behind him. Marty, too, was wearing a black and silver uniform.

Ezekiel strode past Reelys, acknowledging him'er with a nod, and came to a stop directly in front of Vajix!krk.

"I need to speak with you," he said without preamble. "Now."

Something in his face must have told Vajix!krk to accede to his demand. Within a few minutes, they were all in Vajix!krk's office.

"What is it that could not wait till the negotiations were complete, Ezekiel Bones? Even the noble Reelys would say that it was a productive session, and to halt it before we could successfully—"

"I've been studying copies of the Scrolls you have on display," Zeke said.

His words had an immediate effect on the G!at Councilor. She was still and silent for a long minute.

"The reporter," she said at last. "She was your spy all along, was she not? Perhaps I should be thankful she died before any more of our laws could be broken."

Zeke clamped his mouth shut over the angry words that rose up inside him, and held a restraining hand up to Marty, who had taken a threatening step forward.

"Or was it the Councilor?" Vajix!krk continued, turning to face !Jng!xl. "Did she let *you* into the museum as well?"

!Jng!xl hissed softly. "Were you not already involved in one challenge, Councilor, I might engage you in a second for that accusation."

"I beg forgiveness," Vajix!krk said, and even in the harsh, guttural accent of the !xaka!, her words fairly dripped scorn.

"Save the begging," Zeke said, his voice perfectly calm. "Show us the rest of the Scrolls."

Vajix!krk rose up on her third segment and glared down at him.

"You are in no position to make demands! By making copies of the displayed tablets, you have broken an explicit treaty between our two races—and I will bring you before the Galactic Council and charge you with violating that law, I swear it!"

Zeke shook his head. "Making copies of the Scrolls is a violation of no law but your own. Besides, you've broken a higher law by hiding the truth about the tablets!"

"What truth, Ezekiel Bones? What have you discovered in two days that our scientists could not in a hundred years?"

He told her.

"Two different languages?" She made a noise of disgust and dismissal. "That is patent nonsense, Ezekiel Bones. My archaeologists have correctly deciphered the Scrolls—and their interpretation, I might add, is based on a careful examination of all the tablets, not just the paltry few you have studied. And I do not think the Galactic Council would recognize the existence of your 'higher law.' " She pressed a button by the comscreen, and two soldiers entered.

"Escort these four to the antechamber. Ezekiel Bones, our negotiations shall be finished within the next few days. I suggest—no, I insist—you be off-planet, with the slave, at the very minute of their conclusion. Goodbye."

The two soldiers moved forward.

"A moment, Councilor," !Jng!xl began. "I must ask you to reconsider your refusal to let the humans study the remaining tablets."

The soldiers hesitated. Vajix!krk raised a first-segment arm and waved them back.

"On what grounds?"

"Simply these, Councilor," the in!chi said. !Jng!xl crossed the distance between herself and the G!at Councilor so that barely a meter separated them. Watching the sudden confrontation, Zeke was reminded of a chess match, where each individual move was part of some larger strategy. "When Ezekiel Bones came to me with this news, that new light might be shed on our planet's oldest, most revered civilization, I was naturally excited. I disregarded suggestions that the G!at had deliberately obscured and muddied the truth about the N'Gossa. Now, however—what am I to think? What will the other clans think when they hear you will not allow the famed Ezekiel Bones to test the theory he believes to have discovered?"

"It goes without saying that you would inform them of the human's discovery."

"I would feel obliged to, naturally."

Reelys now lowered his'er mouthstalk and spoke for the first time. "Their reactions should be interesting. If they feel they have been lied to—"

"Enough!" Vajix!krk said.

Zeke resisted the urge to smile. This was why he and Marty had told !Jng!xl of their discoveries first—to pressure the G!at Councilor into acceding to their request.

"I am willing to permit you access to the vault where the Scrolls are kept. Tomorrow."

"If you're gonna try something funny. . . ." Marty warned.

"I do not intend anything 'funny,' hlidjski, and if by that you mean to suggest I would consider damaging the Scrolls—"

"It's all right, Marty," Zeke said. "I trust the Councilor to take very good care of the Scrolls. The other clans would never forgive her if something happened to them now."

"Nothing will happen, Ezekiel Bones," Vajix!krk said, "except that your accusations will be proven wrong—and then I will surely bring charges against you to the Galactic Council."

"We'll see," Zeke answered, calmly meeting Vajix!krk's gaze.

She nodded. "An o!xer will meet you at your quarters tomorrow morning."

"At the shuttle station," Zeke corrected, turning to go. "We have to pick up some equipment from our ship. And make it early," he added, allowing the faintest trace of a smile to cross his lips. "I'm anxious to get started."

While Sylvie slept, someone had tended to her wounds. That same someone had brought in a cot for her to sleep on, food and water for her to eat, a blanket to keep her warm. Someone had even had her jumpsuit cleaned and put back on her. And that was disgusting to Sylvie, because as far as she could tell, that someone had to be the G!at.

She had no idea how long she'd been unconscious, how long it had been since the earthquake. A day? A week? She had slept twice more since first awakening in this cell. For all she knew, Marty and Zeke were long gone by now. She couldn't count on any help getting out of here, wherever *here* was. As usual, she was on her own.

But then, that was how she liked being—wasn't it?

Although her mysterious benefactor/captor had dressed the wound on the back of her head, the rest of her body still felt like one giant bruise. She spent five minutes stretching and doing some light calisthenics.

The exercise made her feel good. She drank some water, ate a little of the food the G!at had left her. Then she sat down on the cot and studied her cell again.

The walls and ceiling were made of the same dull gray metal as the floor. All were apparently constructed in one smooth, solid sheet, with no seals, lines, or rivets to be seen. The only break in the monotony came from the circular outlines of a door along one wall. Clearly, that door was the only way out—and no matter how much exercise she did, she wasn't going to be able to knock it down.

That was all right, though: She had already bribed one guard. She could bribe another.

She crossed to the door and banged loudly.

"Hey! Is anybody out there?"

No answer.

"What's going on? Where am I?"

She kicked at the door.

"Damn it, I'm a reporter for United Communications Interplanetary! If you don't let me out of here—"

She tried another tack.

"Listen, if there's anybody out there, I need you to send a message. I can make it very worth your while. . . ."

She waited five full minutes, and not so much as a whisper of sound came from behind that door.

She was clearly going to have to think of another plan.

Outside the cell door, the in!chi warrior charged with guarding her did not stir. Only on explicit order of the Councilor was the door to be opened—or any of the human's questions answered.

"The third and final test," G!daeer announced. "The !dza u!xan—the trial of combat."

It was morning of the next day. For this test, Jackson had not returned to the site of the first two !dza. Instead,

G!daeer had led him—alone—through a series of dimly lit underwater passages until they'd emerged onto what he thought was a patch of ocean floor that had been cleared and flattened.

Then he had looked up, and found himself on the floor of a vast underwater amphitheater. It rose around him in a great circle, a small break in its circumference directly opposite him, with a half-dozen distinctive tiers of seats, designed for an audience separated by caste and clan, no doubt. He also noted the distinctive lights of a repulsor field ringing the arena floor, probably intended to keep the audience in the stands from straying onto the field— or what was in the arena from straying out.

The field was on now.

"I must congratulate you on your performance so far, Jackson Charles," G!daeer was now saying. "It has been a surprise to many of us. But now you face the most difficult challenge of all."

Even through the flat, emotionless voice of the vocoder, Jackson could sense the edge in her words—and if there had been any doubt in his mind before whether or not she knew about the cheating, there was none now. He found himself wondering if—and how—the u!xani would try and cheat on this test. If they did, he had a little surprise of his own planned. He'd grown tired of being one step behind.

Within the underwater arena, the ocean was unnaturally still. Jackson hung motionless in the calm water, barely two meters from G!daeer as she spoke, and could sense again the edge in her words.

"For close to a millennium," the u!xani continued, "!xaka! from all clans have faced their final trial in this manner. Many have failed. But all those who have passed have brought honor and glory to their clans, and made u!xani a name to be reckoned with."

"The u!xani drew their name from the most dangerous predator in Ahng's oceans—a creature of unsurpassed speed and ferocity. The ultimate trial for a u!xani was to defeat this predator in battle—for the victor would then, it was thought, be possessed of all its qualities."

G!daeer click!ed the pincers of her second-segment arms together. A warrior appeared from behind her and handed her a small length of cord.

"For you, Jackson Charles. An attempt to provide you with artificial weapons resembling the !xaka!'s own."

Jackson took the cord from her. He yanked it, testing, and was surprised to feel that its resiliency and strength matched that of the !xaka! webbing that had bound him before.

What was he supposed to do with it?

"Ah," the u!xani said. "The warriors approach—with your opponent."

He turned. Through the murky blue water, he saw a column of u!xani swimming into the amphitheater through its opening opposite him, a large cage floating behind them.

"Behold the u!xan, Jackson Charles," the u!xani said. "Your opponent in this third—and final—!dza."

As the cage drew closer, Jackson got a good long, look at the creature inside it.

Fearsome was the right word; the u!xan was a monster.

Jackson was no expert on evolution, but it seemed to him that the inhospitality of Ahng's frozen surface had forced intelligent life here to develop in a different direction than on Earth. Here, the ability to manipulate one's environment, which on Earth had been bestowed on man and other landdwelling mammals, had evolved in that class of creatures who dwelt on, and within, the ocean floor. On Earth, their closest relatives, though far down the evolutionary ladder, were insects.

The !xaka! themselves were descended from such creatures, and if the closest earth analogue to a !xaka! was the earthworm, then that for the u!xan would have to be the common cockroach. Except this cockroach was a good five meters long. It had six legs, the front pair shorter and more articulated than the others, ending in a fierce-looking set of claws. A brown and gray carapace that looked like, and was probably as hard as, stone protected its body. As Jackson watched, it suddenly roared, the sound echoing through the water around him, and threw itself against the bars of its cage.

He turned back to G!daeer.

"What," he asked simply, "am I supposed to with that?"

"Your task is to subdue the u!xan, and bind its front legs with the coil I have given you."

"Subdue that?" Jackson held up the rope. "With this?"

"Its mandibles have been removed—it cannot harm you, if you are quick enough, and strong enough."

He shook his head. It still looked more than capable of harming him.

"The test will begin when the cage door opens. It will end when you have successfully bound the u!xan, or . . ." she paused significantly, "can no longer continue."

She turned, not bothering to wish Jackson luck, and swam behind the safety of the repulsor fields, where a crowd of u!xani had gathered.

G!daeer must have been controlling the cage door electronically. As soon as she reached the first tier of seats, the door opened.

The u!xan charged out of its cage like a maddened beast, heading straight for Jackson.

He sprang off the arena floor to one side, barely managing to avoid its furious rush. It stopped halfway, smashed into the repulsor field and was bounced off, spilling onto its back. It lay there a second, legs flailing as it struggled to right itself.

Jackson hadn't even had time to think of a strategy—but there was no way he was going to get a better opportunity than this. He dove straight for the creature, holding the rope outstretched in front of him.

As it began to rise, he rammed into it with his shoulder, toppling it over again. At the same time, he looped one end of the rope over a claw, and reached for the other. The u!xan swiped at his arm with its free claw, slicing through the depthsuit and deep into the skin beneath. Jackson slammed his heavy-booted foot into the creature's underbelly, and saw blue-black blood spurt from the sides of the creature's mouth.

I didn't kick it that hard, he thought—and suddenly saw the gaping wounds on either side of its head, where its mandibles must have been removed. The wounds were relatively fresh—no scar tissue had formed yet.

The creature must be in agony. He wondered if the G!at had purposely maimed the beast in this way, to cause it so much pain that it would strike out in rage against whoever came up to it.

What were they going to do with the poor beast now if he defeated it? Put it back in its cage and drag it out again for some other !xaka! to torture?

Jackson was suddenly reminded of the old lion he had tracked on the Serengeti, doomed to live out the days of its life a feeble shadow of its former self.

He knew now Mahsi had been right. He should have killed the lion then.

He thought all this in an instant. Then he reached behind and pulled out the knife he had hidden next to his air tank, and buried it to the hilt in the u!xan's eye.

The creature thrashed wildly, heaving in pain. Great spouts of blood clouded the water. Jackson was upended, sent spinning across the arena.

The u!xan's mouth opened in a final, soundless scream. Then it thrashed once again, and was still.

The u!xan was dead.

And the tests were over.

The warriors in the arena watched him silently. He wondered what they thought of this latest addition to their ranks. And he wondered if the warrior Vajix!krk had chosen was among them.

"You did not pass the test, Jackson Charles!" G!daeer said suddenly, and though her voice was still a monotone, her frenzied clickings betrayed agitation. "You did not obey the rules! You were only to bind the u!xan, not kill it!"

Jackson turned away and began swimming toward the passage he'd entered the arena from.

"Wait, human!" she cried again. "You are not yet u!xani—I have not said you passed the test!"

Jackson didn't bother to turn back.

"You can go to hell," he called out. "And take your damn tests with you."

He disappeared into the underwater tunnels leading back to the Keep.

Chapter Twelve

There were over three hundred tablets in the G!at vaults.

The larger ones weighed about fifteen kilograms, were roughly a meter square, and seven or eight centimeters thick. There were about fifty of those, written in the same language as the *!x'kuta*, what Zeke had taken to referring to as N'Gossa A. The smaller ones were about a quarter of that size, all bearing the script they'd termed N'Gossa B, that so resembled the present-day G!at language.

One by one, Marty had to carry each tablet out of the dank, musty, dim vault where they'd been stored out into a neighboring, brightly lit room. The servos he'd brought down from the *Ostrom* then scanned the tablets' contents and transmitted their images back to Herb, who collated the glyphs with Zeke's previous research. Step by step, they built a vocabulary and transferred it to the remote terminal Zeke now sat at.

It took ten long, tedious, hours to scan each tablet. By the time Marty returned the last one to the vault, two things had been accomplished: they had rough translations for each and every one of the N'Gossa B tablets, and every muscle in his body that hadn't been sore from diving was now sore from the repeated bending and lifting.

But Zeke had gotten no closer to solving the mystery of N'Gossa A.

As the two of them worked, Zeke explained to Marty the path he'd been following in his attempts to decipher the N'Gossa A tablets.

Though their previous work aboard the *Ostrom* made it clear that the two scripts were not identical, they were obviously very closely related. Zeke had begun his research by assuming that the A and B scripts were members of the same linguistic family, using a common set of symbols—the way German and French did, for example.

"Maybe there were two different cultural groups—the priests of ancient N'Gossa, and the unknown writers of N'Gossa A—existing side by side within the ancient city," he said. He'd then assumed that the groups of hiero-glyphs translated as personal pronouns in N'Gossa B would have approximately the same meaning and sen-tence position in N'Gossa A—again, as they did in German and French.

Using those twin hypotheses, he tried translating the *!x'kuta* again . . . and again, came up with nothing.

"Gobbledygook," he told Marty.

When it was clear the two languages were not that closely related, Zeke had embarked on an entirely differ-ent tack.

An inordinately large number of lines in each of the N'Gossa A tablets began with the same group of hieroglyphs. Each of those groups was then followed by a two-glyph phrase that differed throughout the tablet. Zeke tried assuming that each of the two-glyph phrases was simply the declension of the initial glyph pattern.

That hadn't worked either. Nor had a half-dozen other, increasingly convoluted attempts to decipher the *!x'kuta*.

Which brought them up to the present.

Marty yawned, stretching out his arms, trying to work loose the kinks in his arms and back.

"That's the last of the tablets."

Zeke pushed his chair away from the desk, and leaned it back against the wall, crossing his arms behind his head. He yawned himself, then let out a deep sigh of frustration.

"I'm right about this," he said. "I know I am. There's no way the G!at translation for the *!x'kuta* is right—but for the life of me, I can't come up with anything better." He shook his head. "Hell, I can't come up with anything at all."

The strain of the last few hours showed on him. Deep circles lined his eyes, and even Zeke's normally robust skin coloring had paled. He looked exhausted.

"Zeke, you're being a little hard on yourself. To do a translation like this would normally take years."

"Maybe it normally would," he said. "But this isn't a normal situation. We don't have years. We'll be lucky if we have another week."

"We have images of all the tablets now," Marty pointed out. "You can take as much time as you need to examine them—"

"No," Zeke said, shaking his head. "I don't think that would do any good. I have to figure out how these two languages relate to each other."

"Well, we know the two sets of tablets were both found in the same section of the ruins, right?" Marty offered. "And all the tablets are somewhere around two thousand years old—"

Zeke snapped his fingers. "Yes, but how do we know that?" he asked, a light suddenly coming into his eyes. He stood and grabbed a pile of printout off the desk he'd been working at. "For a find this important, doesn't the documentation seem awfully thin?"

"I'd call it pitiful," Marty said. He smiled. "You think the G!at are holding out on us again?"

Zeke waved him off. "No, that's not the issue. Who knows? Maybe they were just incompetent. The point is we're taking a lot of things about these tables for granted. These documents say the tablets are all roughly two thousand years old—but not how that age was arrived at. Did they use mass spectrometry? Carbon-14 dating of the surrounding rock? Or did they just guess? And the fact that they found them in the same section of the ruins—well, what does that mean? Where were they found? In a library, among dozens of other records?" He set the printout down again.

"How are we going to find out?" Marty asked

"Go back to the source," Zeke answered. He picked up a carrysack and shoved the printout and remote terminal inside, then slung it over his shoulder. "Visit the ruins of N'Gossa themselves."

"The ruins—," Marty's voice trailed off. "They're underwater, right?"

Zeke nodded. "Right."

Marty's back began to ache in remembered pain.

"I was afraid you were going to say that," he muttered, shutting down the scanning servos and packing them up.

Vajix!krk could no more refuse them permission to examine the site than she could the tablets—not with !Jng!xl threatening to denounce her before the Diet at this critical juncture. But she warned them that their time at the ruins would be equal to their remaining time on Ahng—and not a moment longer.

"Remaining time on Ahng?" Marty asked, a step behind Zeke as they entered their quarters. "What does she know that we don't?"

"I'll ask Reelys," Zeke said. "Maybe—"

He stopped suddenly. The suite's living room was in darkness. A tall figure stood by the far window, framed by the lights from the Keep. At the sound of their voices, he turned.

"Jackson!" Zeke said, rushing across the room. They hadn't seen each other since Jackson's tests had begun—though of course Zeke had kept track of his progress through Marty and Reelys.

They embraced, and held each other at arm's length. Zeke studied his friend—there was a burn mark along the length of one of his arms, a bruise at the base of his neck, and a large cut along the back of one hand.

Jackson saw him staring, and smiled.

"Momentos," Jackson said ruefully, rubbing the bruise. "They look worse than they feel."

Zeke asked him about the tests.

"Doc," he said wearily. "All I can tell you is—you're looking at the least popular u!xani in history."

Marty came up to him, smiled, and shook his hand. "I knew you could do it." He squinted at Jackson's injuries. "They don't look so bad," Marty said.

"That is because I have been treating him, Marty," Reelys said, floating into the room. "Hello, Ezekiel."

"Reelys—what are you doing here?"

"I have more good news, Ezekiel. A short half-hour ago," the shri said, "the G!at and I successfully completed negotiations for the sale of Kadak!xa. We have agreed on a price—and on what you personally will, and will not do, for the G!at. We will have Kadak!xa back in two days."

"Which is the best news I've had in weeks," Jackson said. "I'm anxious to get out of here. I feel like I could use another fifty years of sleep."

"I'm afraid your role here is not yet ended, Jackson," Reelys said. "We must all appear before the Diet one final time, as if the challenge were going to proceed. The G!at will then announce that they have forfeited their claim to Kadak!xa, citing a desire to preserve interstellar amity, or some similar nonsense. Ezekiel, in recognition of that magnanimous gesture, will then propose compensation for that loss."

"And everybody goes home happy," Jackson said.

"Except that we don't want to go home," Zeke said. "Not in two days, anyway." Now it was his turn to bring Jackson up to date on the Scrolls.

"Would another hand help on that dig, Doc?"

Zeke smiled. "Are you sure you're up to it?"

Jackson nodded.

"Two days! We might as well forget about it," Marty said, kicking at one of the room's strangely shaped pieces of furniture. "That's barely enough time to get started."

Zeke looked at Marty harshly.

"Two days," he said, biting off each word, "is all we've got."

Sylvie had long since shouted herself hoarse. She'd kicked, she'd screamed, threatened United Worlds involvement, offered millions of credits, and nothing had happened. She'd just about given up on the cell door ever opening—when it suddenly dilated, and the last !xaka! she ever expected to see walked in.

"!Jng!xl." She looked around in confusion. "I don't understand."

The Councilor folded her hands, and click!ed the hard edges of her second-segment legs together. They made a sharp noise that echoed throughout the cell.

"What is there not to understand? I am holding you prisoner."

Sylvie's eyes widened in disbelief. The carefully crafted mosaic of events she'd constructed in her mind suddenly fell to pieces. She didn't have enough information yet to form a new one, but one thing was clear. She'd been played for a fool.

"Why?" she asked, backing away from the Councilor, keeping a look of fear and shock on her face. "What do you want me for?" she circled around as she spoke, edging toward the wall, the door, which was still open, and if she could. . . .

!Jng!xl moved further into the cell and motioned to the guard. The door irised shut, and she turned to Sylvie.

"Let us say . . . I believe that you may be of value as a bargaining chip."

Sylvie shook her head. "A bargaining chip? Me? I hardly think I'm of value to anyone. . . ." Her voice trailed off as the meaning of the Councilor's words sunk in.

"Zeke. He's here."

"Not only is he here, he has maneuvered himself rather quickly into a position of power. A position which I may need him to abandon at some point. Hence . . . your continued imprisonment."

Sylvie sat down on the cot, her head spinning.

"Count yourself lucky to be alive, Sylvie Pharr. When my warrior found you, you were half-dead, buried beneath a layer of rubble," !Jng!xl said.

"Why'd you bother rescuing me?"

"It was truly no bother—it took very little effort on my part, and at the time, I had visions of supplying you with information for another article. Information that would reveal how the G!at seemed determined to force the coming clan war."

Sylvie remembered the Councilor's o!xer, who had been so helpful in taking her to the comm station. "You read my article."

!Jng!xl inclined her head in acknowledgement. "I am the only one so far—though perhaps I will show that hidden message to Ezekiel Bones as proof that you are my prisoner."

Sylvie raised her eyes suddenly and met !Jng!xl's impassive gaze with her own fierce stare.

"You hurt Zeke, and I'll kill you."

!Jng!xl made a noise then, one Sylvie had never heard before, but knew instantly what it was. A laugh.

"Be thankful I haven't killed *you* yet, Sylvie Pharr. And hope your friend Ezekiel Bones does nothing which makes that necessary."

The ruins of ancient N'Gossa, rumored by the news agencies to be one of the galaxy's great unexplored archaeological sites, were a bit of a letdown at first.

In point of fact, they were almost invisible.

Zeke was disappointed; he had been hoping for something more spectacular—like the abandoned tetrahedral shells on Aston-3, or Earth's own drowned city of Port Royal.

Marty shared his feelings.

"This is it?" he asked. He sat between Zeke and Jackson in the floatcar. All three were staring through the car's transparent shell. Two G!at u!xani, who had accompanied them to the site at Vajix!krk's insistence, were at the controls. "These are the ruins of N'Gossa?"

"Where?" Jackson asked. "I can't see a thing."

Zeke showed Jackson where to look, not at all surprised by his inability to see the ruins—it was difficult enough for him, a trained observer, to pick out the ancient city's buildings and monuments, now hidden by plant growth and the accumulation of silts and sediments.

On the one hand, Zeke was glad to see the comparatively undisturbed overgrowth. It would make dating the tablets much easier—*if* the G!at archaeologists had noted the discovery sites correctly. On the other hand . . . working on digs like this one demanded a tedious, methodological approach—and they only had two days.

They were going to need an awful lot of luck to get any conclusive findings.

Their floatcar drew up to a grouping of prefabricated pressure domes, and docked with one. Inside the dome, they unpacked all the equipment and servos Marty had brought down from the *Ostrom* and donned depth-suits. The two u!xani leading, Zeke and his team emerged into Ahng's cool, freshwater ocean.

The first thing Zeke noticed was something that he'd missed coming in by floatcar—the domes were set on a rocky, rubble-strewn slope that curved gently upward to the ice-covered surface of Ahng's oceans and then disappeared. Above the ice was the slope's true peak—the G!at shuttle station.

As they swam closer, details began to take shape: the outline of a broad plaza here, the fallen columns of a large building there. None of this would have been visible without the efforts of the G!at archaeologists who had come before them. But the ruins roused no sense of discovery in Zeke. He didn't get the feeling that the site had ever been anything special, certainly not in the way the legends described the N'Gossa.

Then the u!xani leading them swam past the edge of the ruins and disappeared into the side of the rocky slope. Exchanging puzzled glances, they followed.

Zeke saw now that the u!xani had actually entered a half-submerged structure of some kind, and were burrowing a path for themselves, flinging earth and rock in their wake. When the way was clear, they motioned them forward.

They passed through the entranceway and downward into a small cave, clogged with rubble. Directly opposite them, at the far end of the cave, a pale blue light gleamed through a circular opening in the wall.

"N'Gossa," one u!xani said through her vocoder, waving them forward. She disappeared through the circular opening.

Marty looked at Zeke. Jackson looked at Zeke. Zeke tried not to look puzzled.

"I thought you said that," Jackson said, pointing to the ruins above him, "was N'Gossa."

"I thought it was," Zeke said, excitement suddenly mounting within him. "Let's go," he said, swimming forward. "Lights on."

Two of the servos they'd brought down from the *Ostrom*, constructed to resemble fish, darted ahead to flank him. Each was equipped with camera "eyes" and a high intensity spotlight for a "mouth." At Zeke's command, those spotlights now flashed on, illuminating a path for him toward the pale blue luminescence.

"Where's that coming from?" Marty wondered.

As he spoke, Zeke passed through the circular opening—and caught his breath.

Here, now, were the true ruins of N'Gossa.

"My God," he said. "Look at it."

Before him stretched a single, huge cave. Its roof was the ocean floor above, its bottom a rock-strewn plain fifty meters below them. And all up and down the cavern walls were thousands of circular openings, just like the one he'd come from, the one Marty and Jackson were now wriggling through.

The pale blue light he'd noticed before came from a luminescent plant growth, some kind of algae perhaps, that covered the cavern walls, casting an eerie glow over the entire scene.

In that first split second, as Zeke gazed upon the ruins of ancient N'Gossa, he pictured the city as it must have looked two thousand years ago.

The circular openings were handsomely decorated archways then, the dwelling places of the N'Gossa. The rockstrewn plain had probably been the city center, the original site of the Great Hall and dozens of other buildings like it. Zeke knew instantly that the G!at had no connection with this underwater city—its open architecture would have been anathema to their rigid, constricting rules of order. And he also knew why the G!at had stopped exploration of the site a hundred years ago—for the very same reason.

Their connection with the race that built these ruins was a sham.

"Doc," Jackson said, tugging him on the arm. "You all right?"

"What? Oh, yes, yes I'm fine." He turned back to the servos and ordered them to start recording.

"I hope we have enough time to film all this," Marty said.

"Not a chance," Zeke said, shaking his head. "Come on, let's get to work."

Following the u!xani before them, they swam down toward the floor of the cave.

The forces that had destroyed the ancient city were far more evident on the cavern floor. Massive blocks of stone and metal lay everywhere, and toward the back of the cavern, huge outcroppings of rock had been thrust upward above the ocean floor.

The u!xani led them around one of the outcrops to the site where the tablets had been found.

Marty took one look and exhaled in disgust.

The G!at, to be charitable, had left the place a mess.

There were actually two separate digging pits, about ten meters apart. The u!xani identified one as the site where the N'Gossa A tablets had been found, the other as the N'Gossa B site. Both were contained within the rough outlines of a building that, when standing, must have rivaled the Great Hall in sheer size. Many of the blocks of stone strewn about nearby had probably come from it.

The pits themselves were in roughly the same condition as that building. Ruined. Neither site had been fortified anywhere near strongly enough, and both the fortifications that had been built and the sides of the pits themselves had actually fallen in and clogged the digging pits. No filters of any kind had been set up either, which meant that sediments and all sorts of debris had been collecting within the pits for the last fifty years.

He couldn't say for sure that the G!at had deliberately fouled up the dig—but he'd rarely seen incompetence on such a high scale.

"We're not going to get anything useful out of here unless we spend a month cleaning up first, Zeke," Marty said.

Zeke shook his head. "We don't have a month. We have two days."

"Then we're gonna need a miracle."

"Well, the first thing we're gonna need to do is dig, right?" Jackson swam before the two of them, and held there, treading water. "Clear these pits?"

"That's right," Zeke said.

"Okay, then," Jackson said. He unzipped the large carrysack he'd been holding, and pulled out several small digging servos. Activating them, he set half to work in each pit.

"I'm going to take a look around," Marty said. "Let me know when the pits are clear."

He swam away from them, heading further back into the cavern.

"How did this place manage to stay undiscovered for so long?" Jackson asked.

"I think that probably has a lot to do with how the city was destroyed," Zeke said, watching the servos begin ferrying the larger pieces of debris out of the pits. Once they had the way mostly clear, he intended to step in and do the more delicate work himself. "Legend has it N'Gossa sank beneath the sea because of a giant cataclysm—an earthquake, or something like that. If there were no survivors, maybe no one would have known where to look for it."

"Earthquakes do seem to be a pretty regular occurrence around here," Jackson said. "But that one would have had to have been pretty big. Powerful enough to affect not only the surrounding area, but maybe even the entire planet— so that even those who knew about the city were hit."

A small beeping sound over the comm unit indicated that the servos working in one of the pits were nearing the end of their task. Zeke swam over, and looked in.

The G!at dig here—where the N'Gossa B tablets had been found—was only about five meters square, and they hadn't had to go very far down to find the tablets.

It was shallow enough that they just might get lucky, and be able to get an accurate dating on some of the rocks. The G!at dig had exposed a fairly discernable bedding—the top layer appeared to be pretty standard undersea muck, but beneath that, the soil appeared much darker, almost black, in fact. . . .

"They're done with the big stuff in the other pit, Doc," Jackson called out over the comm channel.

"Got that, Marty?" Zeke said. "The pits are clear. I'm going to start taking samples."

"Be there in a minute," the hlidjski's voice came back, sounding as excited as Zeke had ever heard him get. "There's a really strange collection of rocks back here. Shale, limestone, obsidian. . . ."

"Save the exploring for later," Zeke said. "We need you here now."

"Right—be with you in a sec." They heard his comm channel switch off.

Zeke swam back and forth between the two pits. The first, where the N'Gossa A tablets had been found, was much larger, and was located in the center of the ruined building. The N'Gossa B pit was located near the edge of it.

"This is weird, Zeke," Marty said, swimming over to them. In each of his hands he held a rock. "Look. This"—he held up the rock in his right hand—"is shale, and this"—he held up his other hand—"is a chunk of pumice, embedded in a basalt flow."

"Pumice?" Jackson asked. "I'm no geologist, but isn't that some kind of lava?"

"You bet," Marty said.

"So what does that mean?" Zeke asked.

"Well . . . I'm not entirely sure." Marty said hesitantly, fingering the rock. "I want to take a few samples from the back of the cavern before I commit myself to anything."

"All right," Zeke said finally. "But don't take too long. We really do need you here."

"Right," Marty said. He grabbed one of the digging servos and swam away excitedly.

If Marty had found something interesting, all well and good, but he didn't want to lose sight of the reason they were down here. The Scrolls, after all, were the important thing.

He set to work taking samples.

Zeke turned out to be wrong about the relative importance of Marty's explorations.

About halfway through the day, he and Marty returned to the *Ostrom* with their samples, leaving Jackson behind with the servos to continue collecting more data. They went to the main lab and immediately began an analysis of the strata the two groups of tablets had been found in.

Reelys, who didn't have much inclination for geology, even volunteered to help, and Marty gleefully set him to work dating samples, happy, for once, to know more than the shri about something.

In less than an hour, Zeke was certain his initial guess had been right.

The G!at's connection with ancient N'Gossa was a lie.

The tablets written in N'Gossa A were on the order of two thousand years older than the N'Gossa B tablets. Except for the symbols they used, the two languages were completely unrelated. To Zeke, it seemed as if the G!at's ancestors had simply stumbled onto the original tablets and used those symbols to create their own language.

The supposed *!x'kuta*, of course, were a complete fabrication.

Preliminary correlations between a number of different rock beddings they'd found also indicated that the ruins, including the Great Hall, were contemporaneous with the N'Gossa A tablets, not the N'Gossa B.

So the G!at, who claimed to be descended from their planet's first civilization, were in fact, little more than scavengers who had once dwelt among its ruins. And their language was nothing but a degenerate version of the original N'Gossa tongue.

"I would not accuse the G!at of deliberately covering up the truth about their past before we are safely back aboard the *Ostrom* with Kadak!xa aboard, Ezekiel," Reelys said after Zeke told him'er. "Or we may find ourselves in the middle of a whole new set of negotiations."

"I don't intend to accuse them of anything," Zeke said, smiling. "I'll just pass along the evidence I've gathered to !Jng!xl."

Reelys held out a chart of the latest sample s/he had dated from the N'Gossa A pit. Zeke studied it carefully, noting that it was the third straight such sample they had dated at between 1500 and 2000 years old.

He'd found some other surprises among the ruins as well; one in particular had struck him. In some small but significant ways, the original N'Gossans had been physically different from present-day !xaka!. Images of some of the oldest cave dwellings, with their small, twisting entrances, suggested to him that the N'Gossans were smaller, more flexible. . . .

In the far corner of the lab, Marty suddenly burst out laughing.

"What's so funny?" Zeke asked.

"I may have some other information for you to pass along," Marty called out. He was studying some of the images the servos had taken of his rocks. "Got a second?"

Zeke and Reelys both crossed the room.

"See this?" Marty said, pointing to one of the images he'd had Herb blow up. It showed a stack of grayish, sack-like rocks spread out along the cavern floor. "This is called pillow lava. You find it, generally speaking, wherever underwater volcanic eruptions occur. But I've never seen it in such quantities, anywhere."

"What's it doing inside an underwater cave?" Zeke said.

"I was asking myself that question about two hours ago," Marty said. "So I decided to have another look at the images we took of the cavern as we entered."

He pulled out another three or four images from the stack on his desk and spread them out for Zeke and Reelys to look at.

"The stuff is everywhere," Zeke said.

"Even on the walls," Marty nodded. "And that's when I figured it out. This underwater cavern is what we technically refer to as a lava cave."

"A what?" Reelys asked.

"A lava cave. They're formed when the source of a below-ground lava stream is suddenly cut off. The remaining lava contracts, and you're left with a big empty space . . . a lava cave. And this," he pointed again at the image of the cavern, "is the granddaddy of all lava caves."

Reelys fluttered his'er tentacles in excitement. "The presence of so much lava requires a very big volcano, does it not Marty?"

"Not necessarily—but in this case, it certainly does," he said. "That's what we have to tell the !xaka! about." He laughed. "Herb, show us the images above the lava cave."

The computer complied, and the viewscreen on the far wall filled with the image of the ruins as they'd first seen them from the floatcar, and the pressure domes on the long, sloping hill leading up to the shuttle station.

"See?" Marty asked.

Zeke shook his head. "I'm afraid I don't."

"All right," Marty replied. "Hold on a minute." He manipulated the image on the viewscreen, turning it sideways, pulling back the perspective, and extrapolating the shape of the rest of the island.

When he was done, there was a picture of a flat-topped mountain on the screen, most of it underwater. The lava cave was located directly at its base, and the shuttle station on its summit.

Zeke stared at it for a moment.

"See?" Marty said. "Those idiots built their shuttle station right on top of a volcano."

Zeke suddenly realized what the almost black layers of soil in the pits had been.

Ash, from the volcano's previous eruptions.

"That ties in with what I've found," Zeke said. "One of these eruptions must have happened about four thousand years ago—that's where the N'Gossa A tablets were buried. The next and most recent one happened two thousand years ago. The N'Gossa B site."

Reelys's mantle shimmered, and his'er mouthstalk lowered again. "That is an interesting pattern," s/he said. "Major eruptions every two thousand years—approximately."

"Approximately," Marty said. He looked up at Zeke. "You say the last one happened . . . ?"

"Two thousand years ago," Zeke repeated.

"Well?" Reelys asked. "What does that suggest?"

Zeke looked over at the image of the volcano, and then back at Marty.

"Trouble," he said.

Chapter Thirteen

Zeke forgot all about trying to decipher the N'Gossa A tablets. When Jackson notified him that the servos had uncovered a number of possible treasures in the course of taking some further soil samples, he reluctantly ordered those set aside for further study as well.

If they only had a day left here, it was clear what his priorities had to be.

So even though geology wasn't his real field of expertise, Zeke worked through the night with Marty, running spectroscopy tests on the samples they'd brought back, helping him analyze and date the different layers of strata they'd uncovered among the ruins. Several of those layers contained rocks too fine grained to have formed from any-thing but lava flows or ash deposits—more evidence of past cataclysms. Many of the strata also contained crystalline deposits, usually formed by similar volcanic processes.

The servos, under Jackson's supervision, continued to beam back images from the site. Herb weeded through those images as they were transmitted and printed out the best ones for Zeke, who in turn passed along the ones he thought of value to Marty.

Marty was right, of course—they were doing all this far too quickly to be entirely sure of their facts. But as their work progressed, it became clear he was on target.

The shuttle station was built on top of an active volcano—and there was a pretty fair chance it would erupt sometime within the next few years, possibly a whole lot sooner. And when it went, it was going to take with it the shuttle station and a good-sized chunk of N'Gossa Island itself.

It seemed worth telling the G!at about.

A few hours after nightfall, Zeke told Jackson to collect the servos and call it a day. He and Marty spent another few hours gathering their data and putting it into a form Vajix!krk would be able to comprehend.

They slept that night onboard the *Ostrom*, rose early the next morning, and, after contacting Reelys to tell him'er of their plans, took the shuttle down to N'Gossa again. Zeke had a nervous moment as they were descending—visions of the volcano choosing that instant to explode and blow them and the shuttle station completely off the planet kept running through his head—but they landed without incident.

Their first stop was the in!chi consular tower, next to the Great Hall. Zeke feared that the G!at would order them off the planet immediately after the ceremony today ended, no matter what their reaction to his news about the volcano. So he had brought along proof to show !Jng!xl that the G!at's claim of descent from the N'Gossa was false.

Only she wasn't there.

"The Councilor left early this morning, Ezekiel Bones, on business I, unfortunately, was not privy too," one of her o!xer told them. "However, I am sure she plans to be at the Diet this afternoon."

Zeke thanked the o!xer, and decided against leaving the material with her.

Their next stop was Vajix!krk's office in the nearby
G!at consular tower. Two u!xani stood guard, one outside
the Councilor's door, and another inside, who wore the
clan symbol of the in!chi. The latter moved aside to let
them pass as they entered.

"Councilor," Zeke began, bowing. "I have important
news for you."

"And I for you, Ezekiel Bones," Vajix!krk said, rising
to greet them. She had been engaged in conversation
with another !xaka!, who remained seated on one of the
floor cushions in her office, her back to them. A number
of bowls and serving flasks had been set out for the two
!xaka!, indicating some kind of formal conference, or
celebration.

"My o!xer have located the informant who told us of
your slave's impending arrival—and with the aid of the
in!chi"—the other !xaka rose and bowed slightly to him
now, and Zeke saw it was !Jng!xl—"we have uncovered
those who changed the message sent to your slave." There
was a hint of satisfaction in her voice as she spoke. "The
!van are responsible. It appears that they had hoped to
engage the two of us in meaningless conflict over the
slave, making the G!at appear to be—the word is *bullies*,
I believe."

He and Marty exchanged skeptical glances. Zeke
decided to accept the Councilor's word at face value—
after all, the whirlwind of events the last few days, coupled with the deal Reelys had arranged, had made the
whole issue of who had lured Kadak!xa here seem somewhat remote and unimportant.

"I guess I owe you an apology then, Councilor," he said
to Vajix!krk. "This whole mess turns out to be . . . not
entirely your fault." He couldn't quite bring himself to

say that the G!at were blameless—after all, they were responsible for seizing Kadak!xa.

And in a sense, for Sylvie's death.

"Apology accepted, Ezekiel Bones," the G!at Councilor responded. "When the Diet meets this morning I shall present the evidence we have gathered—and demand reparations from the !van Councilor for this." Vajix!krk indicated the refreshments that had been laid out for herself and !Jng!xl. "Please help yourselves."

Zeke studied the assortment dubiously and shook his head. He held up the packet of information they'd brought along.

"You should take a look at this before you plan any long celebrations," he said.

Vajix!krk hiss/click!ed irritably. "What is it now, Ezekiel Bones? Have you made some other tremendous discovery about our past—or perhaps," she said, leaning forward and speaking more intently, "you have come here to tell me that you were wrong about the Scrolls?"

"Actually, the first," Zeke said. He handed her one of the two folders he was carrying. The other, of course, was for !Jng!xl, but he'd wait to give her that. "Take a look— I think you'll find it of a lot more immediate interest than the Scrolls were."

Vajix!krk crossed to a work-station on the far wall and set the folder down in front of her. She opened it, and began scanning through the images and information they'd gathered.

!Jng!xl lowered herself back onto one of the cushions, unconcerned with what the humans had now found.

Her plans had worked to perfection. It had been a simple matter to direct the G!at o!xer to the informant, and just as simple to direct the trail of investigation to the

!van Councilor, who had already withdrawn from the Keep, infuriated by the G!at's accusations. With luck, the Diet might even vote to censure the !van.

She would then have nothing to do but sit back and wait for the inevitable war to unfold.

Oh, yes. Seeing Ezekiel Bones reminded her that the reporter would now have to be disposed of as well.

!Jng!xl scanned the many bowls of delicacies the G!at Councilor had ordered set out for their meeting, finally selecting a *b'steri*, one of the more exotic crystalline nuggets. She peeled off the outer layer with a knife, and popped the nugget into her undermouth, letting the sweet, thick interior dissolve slowly in her mouth.

She leaned back on the cushion, savoring the taste.

"This is ridiculous, Ezekiel Bones," Vajix!krk said, throwing the folder aside. "Our scientists have studied the volcano for years—there is no evidence of any activity whatsoever."

"Then how do you explain the quakes you've been having?" Zeke asked.

"As I told you, they are a fact of life here on Ahng." The Councilor rose and handed the folder back to Zeke. "I thank you for your concern, but we have constructed the Keep to withstand such minor tremors. It will last a thousand years."

"I wouldn't bet on that," Marty said. "That volcano"—he waved a hand at the window, and the shuttle station in the distance—"could blow any minute. And when it does, this whole island—and your Keep—are going with it."

"Such cataclysms are the stuff of legends," Vajix!krk said, waving him away. "It is too fantastic."

"These aren't legends," Zeke said, pulling out one of the images—a rough stratigraphic sequence of the bedding within the lava cave—and waving it in the air. "These are facts. Have your scientists take a look at them."

"Excuse me—Ezekiel Bones," !Jng!xl said. "May I see the data?"

Zeke shoved the whole folder at her.

"Here—maybe you can talk some sense into the Councilor," he said.

!Jng!xl studied the documents a moment.

And quite suddenly, the war she had planned so long seemed unnecessary.

"The evidence does seem convincing," she said, looking up at Zeke. "Unless drastic measures are taken, you say, the entire island is doomed?"

"That's about the size of it," Marty answered. "We have to start evacuating now, or the G!at are going into the history books right next to the N'Gossa under 'lost civilizations.'"

"You think the humans are correct, Councilor?" Vajix!krk asked, a note of uncertainty creeping into her voice.

"They may be." She turned to Zeke. "Has anyone else seen this data?"

"No," Zeke said. "We haven't had time to finish compiling everything we've found yet."

"Excellent." !Jng!xl rose slowly from the cushion, and spoke to the u!xani by the door. "!Dana."

The warrior bowed, and came forward.

!Jng!xl waved a first-segment hand. "Kill the G!at."

Vajix!krk rose. "Councilor, is this some sort of joke?" She rose up on her third segment and studied the approaching u!xani. "I warn you, I am in no mood for—"

The u!xani reared back, and in one precise, practiced motion of her bladed leg, cut Vajix!krk open along the joint between her first and second segments.

The G!at Councilor shuddered and gasped, her many legs and arms flailing helplessly. She toppled forward onto the table of refreshments. The bowls of delicacies spilled onto the floor, mingling together with the Councilor's own lifeblood.

Vajix!krk shuddered once more, and was still.

!Jng!xl turned to Zeke and Marty, who stood frozen with shock.

"My God," Zeke croaked, his voice hoarse with astonishment. "Why?"

"Why?" !Jng!xl said. "That should be obvious. I am ensuring that this eruption that is to come destroys not only the Keep, but the power of the clan G!at. Forever."

Jackson almost slept through the whole thing.

He'd neglected to ask the room computer for a wake-up call the night before—not too surprising, considering how exhausted he'd been when he came in. He'd spent almost twenty hours underwater supervising Marty's army of servos as they rooted around the ruins, surfacing only to change airtanks and eat. So it was no wonder he slept soundly, oblivious even to the insistent pounding on his door.

He was awakend by the sound of someone rooting through his bags. At first, he thought he was being robbed.

He cracked open his eyes warily, and saw Reelys floating at the foot of his bed, a different article of Jackson's clothing in each of his'er tentacles.

"Wake up, Jackson. You must get dressed quickly, or we will be late for the Diet."

Jackson yawned. "What time is it? Where's Zeke?"

"It is late. Ezekiel and Marty have gone ahead to speak with the G!at Councilor in private—you must hurry, Jackson," Reelys said. S/he held out Jackson's coverall with one tentacle, and began pulling down his blankets with another.

"Hey," Jackson said, grabbing the blanket back. "Would you mind? I don't usually get dressed in front of strangers."

Reelys bent an eyestalk quizzically.

"I'm not wearing any clothes now," Jackson said.

"And you don't wish me to see you in this state?" Reelys asked.

"That's right," Jackson said, feeling his face flush.

"But I am not wearing any clothes, Jackson," Reelys pointed out. "And I am letting you observe me—"

"It's different," Jackson said.

Reelys bobbed up and down at the edge of the bed. "Many humans in the Legion observed the same custom," s/he said. "Although as a doctor—"

"Look, will you just let me get dressed?"

Reelys let Jackson's clothes fall on the bed and turned to go. "Perhaps you will let me see you unclothed another time."

Jackson got dressed quickly, afraid that Reelys would pop back in at any moment.

An o!xer arrived and escorted them to one of the G!at Councilor's private floatcars. Jackson spent the entire trip listening to the shri lecture on the comparative merits of !xaka!ian and human monumental architecture.

He could see why Marty sometimes felt Reelys was a bit annoying.

Finally, they arrived at the Great Hall. This time, the galleries were empty, and only four Councilors were seated at the dais.

Zeke and Marty weren't there either.

"Where are they?" Jackson asked.

"Calm yourself, Jackson," Reelys said. "Notice that the G!at Councilor has not arrived yet either. They are undoubtedly still in conference together."

Jackson nodded silently.

The door behind them dilated, and a column of G!at soldiers entered. Kadak!xa was with them.

And so was the u!xani Vajix!krk had chosen as champion.

And there was G!daeer as well. It was just like old home week.

Jackson swallowed hard.

He was beginning to get a very bad feeling about all this. . . .

The grisly tableau remained unchanged. Vajix!krk lay sprawled across the table, the bowls of delicacies now coated with blood and gore. The u!xani stood next to Zeke and Marty, who were watching !Jng!xl destroy the last of the papers they had brought.

She'd also found the other folder Zeke was carrying, the one that described in minute detail how the G!at ancestors had faked their descent from the N'Gossans.

"It was very thoughtful for you to bring this to me as well, Ezekiel Bones. Perhaps, if any of the G!at survive the upcoming cataclysm, this will prove useful."

"I hope you choke on it," Marty said.

The u!xani hissed.

"I do owe you two a debt of thanks," !Jng!xl said. "Your presence here was only supposed to be an annoyance, a wedge with which to drive the feuding clans further apart. Instead, you have provided me with the information for a much more spectacular achievement: the complete and utter destruction of the clan G!at."

Zeke had a sudden, blinding realization. "It was *you*" he said. "You changed the message."

!Jng!xl bowed.

"You can't let all the !xaka! on this island die!" Zeke said. "You have to release that information."

"Why should the deaths of ten million G!at bother me? It is far less than would have died in the war I planned, and it will serve my purposes just as well."

"So would releasing the information on the Scrolls," Marty said. "Or hadn't you thought of that?"

"Of course I had," !Jng!xl said, lowering all eight segments of her massive body to the floor. She crossed the room and deposited the remains of the first folder in a wall slot.

"But this explosion, when it comes, will result in not only the physical destruction of the G!at citadel, but in the destruction of all their records—financial, economic, historical—everything. It shall be a blow the clan can never recover from."

"And what do you plan on doing with us?" Zeke asked.

"Ah," !Jng!xl lowered herself onto one of the cushions near the serving table and pushed Vajix!krk's body aside. She popped another nugget into her mouth.

"I will summon the G!at o!xer, who will enter to this tragic scene. I will be deeply shaken as I explain the morning's events.

"You came here in a last-minute attempt to change the terms of your agreement with the Councilor. She refused—you grew angry, and used this knife"—she picked up one of the carving blades off the table—"to kill her. My guard then had no choice but to kill you."

She motioned to the u!xani.

"!Dana?"

The warrior hissed, and moved forward.

"We must do this quickly," !Jng!xl said, "before the Councilor's blood grows cold, and clots."

Chapter Fourteen

"Councilors," Reelys said. S/he had waited as long as possible for Vajix!krk and Ezekiel to aririve and complete their transaction, but could not delay any longer.

The fools were actually going to force Jackson to fight.

Changing his'er mantle pattern from red to blue, a color the !xaka! considered high-caste, and inflating to his'er full stature, Reelys began to speak.

"I must inform you that negotiations between the G!at and Ezekiel Bones for the sale of Kadak!xa have been successfully completed. The ceremony today was not to be this combat, but the transaction of that offer."

S/he spoke only to the !seri, Ghi!reeli, and !xamini Councilors. The !van representative had apparently withdrawn from the city—some sort of allegation by the G!at, s/he had been led to understand—but Reelys was surprised not to see !Jng!xl here now. The in!chi was at least capable of independent, rational thought—whereas the three who now occupied the dais seemed to him'er mere puppets for the larger alliances.

"Forgiveness, noble shri," the Ghi!reeli Councilor said, "but I have heard nothing of these negotiations. Surely you do not mean to suggest that my close ally, the G!at Councilor, would not inform me of them?"

"All respect—I must concur with my colleague," the !seri Councilor stated. "We have no reason to believe the fight is not simply to proceed as planned."

"Is my word not enough?" Reelys hissed angrily.

The Councilors fell all over each other trying to apologize.

"We do not mean to imply—"

"Forgiveness—"

"Of course we believe you are speaking truthfully—"

Fools, Reelys thought. S/he had a sudden, irrational impulse to ascend the dais and inform the Councilors there that the shri would now take responsibility for running their affairs, as they obviously did not have the intellectual wherewithal to give orders to a bladderwort.

Jackson motioned Reelys over.

"Where are they?" he asked between gritted teeth.

"Clearly, I have no more idea than you do," Reelys told him.

"Look, I'm in no shape to fight. I've just spent a whole day digging up rocks—"

"Please," Reelys said, allowing a touch of exasperation to creep into his'er voice. The strain of dealing with !xaka! for so long . . . it was making him'er less than diplomatic to others as well. S/he decided a long period of rest would be necessary once affairs here were concluded. "There is no need for you to list your ailments. I have no intention of allowing the fight to take place, nor do these"—she searched for an appropriate term and failed to find one—"*Councilors* have the power to force it."

On the dais, the Councilors had just finished talking among themselves. Now the Ghi!reeli spoke. "We do not mean to doubt your word, noble Reelys, however—"

"We will not fight," Reelys said. "And you will be deliberately going against the wishes of the G!at Councilor if you force this challenge to proceed. Simply wait another few moments—"

"We have waited long enough," the !xamini Councilor said. "The fight must take place now. The Diet has many important matters to consider today, and we can waste no more time on this one."

Incredible. In just one short session, these three had developed a vastly overrated sense of their own importance. And even more incredible—at this time they were, for all intents and purposes, the planet's ruling body.

"You cannot force the challenge to proceed," Reelys said. "Neither of the parties is directly present."

The Councilors fell silent. They had no ready answer to that objection.

But another did.

"The u!xani is here, shri," G!daeer said. She stood in front of the warrior Vajix!krk had chosen as champion.

Reelys was startled. G!daeer had spoken directly to him—an incredible breach of protocol. But none of her superiors moved to admonish her.

"I am ready to fight," the u!xani champion stated, turning to face Jackson Charles. "I risk my honor for my clan, human. I risk my life. Will you not do the same?"

Jackson stared stonily ahead, but did not speak.

"Are you u!xani, human?" G!daeer hissed. "Or a coward?"

"We will not fight," Reelys said.

"Then we have no choice," the Ghi!reeli Councilor said. "We declare the challenge withdrawn, and custody of the slave—"

"Wait." Jackson stepped forward.

"Jackson!" Reelys hissed. "What are you doing?"

"It's all right," Jackson said. He looked up to the Councilors on the dais. "I'll fight."

Reelys's mantle shimmered, changing colors quickly from blue to a darker, more metallic sheen. "Jackson, this ruling does not matter. Once the G!at appear, we can appeal, have it overturned—"

"No," Jackson said firmly. Maybe Reelys was a lot smarter than he was, but Jackson had just seen the G!at u!xani cheat and lie and even attempt to kill him during the tests. He wouldn't depend on them for anything. Especially when it concerned someone's life.

He glanced over at Kadak!xa, who sat directly behind and to the left of the dais in the gallery of the Great Hall, closely guarded. She was watching him now, dejection and defeat etched in her body posture. He guessed her opinion of the G!at's dependability matched his.

"No," he repeated. "If the Diet awards the G!at custody, we'll never see Kadak!xa again. I know it."

For a moment, Reelys seemed taken aback by his sudden passion. Then s/he exhaled audibly, and placed a sensory tentacle on Jackson's shoulder. An eyestalk bent up, and stared directly at him.

"You will not wait for Ezekiel, Jackson?"

Jackson laid his hand over Reelys's tentacle.

"Something's happened to him, Reelys, or he'd be here now."

Reelys deflated visibly. "If I cannot change your mind . . . then I will wish you luck."

"You're talking to the divinely lucky Jackson Charles, remember?" he said, attempting to lighten the mood. "The u!xani's going to need the help."

While they had spoken, an area in front of the dais had been cleared. Several o!xer carried out a large carpet and unrolled it across the floor. It was a sea of violets and blues, and in its center, embroidered in gold and black, was the clan symbol of the G!at. Several small, darker patches also stained its surface.

It had apparently been used for challenges before.

An o!xer guided Jackson to one corner of the carpet, and the u!xani to another.

Jackson began a series of stretching exercises, trying to work out the massive knots in his shoulders and neck he'd gotten from diving yesterday. He felt mentally unprepared to fight as well; the morning's haphazard and unexpected events had robbed him of his usual equilibrium.

He was also a little scared.

As he'd told Zeke, Jackson had fought and killed a !xaka! once before. But that one had been a slave—lower-caste, uneducated, untrained. His opponent now was u!xani—a warrior, bred to battle, its entire body a weapon. Still, his strategy had to be the same. A quick, killing strike, before the !xaka! could use its formidable natural weaponry.

He finished stretching, and indicated his readiness to the o!xer. She and the u!xani exchanged a series of clicks.

"Begin," the o!xer called out.

The Hall was almost silent, quiet enough so that the only sounds Jackson could hear were his own breathing and that of his opponent. He paced the edges of the carpet, out of range of the !xaka!'s spinnerets.

The u!xani hissed, and lifted to reveal its bladed second-segment leg. It waved the blade back and forth in the air several times, the cutting edge gleaming in the light.

Jackson circled, looking for an opening.

Zeke inched slowly backward, his right hand stretched out behind him. His fingers ran along the shelves next to the wall, searching. . . .

And closed on the object they'd been seeking.

!Dana moved toward him, raised up on her third segment, bladed leg held high. An opening on one side of her body dilated.

"Move!" Zeke yelled. He shoved Marty in one direction, toward the door, and dived in the other himself. A spray of acid shot past him, its fumes singeing his nose. The acid struck one of the wall etchings, which began to smoke and dissolve.

Zeke had time for a brief pang of anger and loss as he watched two thousand years of history disappear. Then he had to dive again, as another burst of acid shot by him.

He rolled to his feet. Behind !Dana, Marty had almost reached the door, and escape.

"The hlidjski!" !Jng!xl called out.

!Dana spun quickly. From another opening on her body, a strand of webbing shot out, and caught Marty around the chest. He clawed at it futilely, trying to tear it off him. Another strand shot out, and caught him around the ankle.

!Dana jerked that second strand backward.

Marty slammed into the floor, face first, and lay still.

The u!xani turned to Zeke.

Zeke retreated again, till the window was at his back, and he could go no further.

!Jng!xl hiss/click!ed in satisfaction.

!Dana reared back, poised to strike.

Zeke whipped the !kan out from down at his side, where he had hidden it, and in one swift motion, sprung its blades and charged.

He was no expert with the weapon—he hadn't even been sure he'd be able to open it. But there was one way to use it he was sure would work.

Using both hands, he swung the !kan like a pickaxe, burying one of its blades deep into !Dana's soft underbelly. With all his strength, he ripped upward. He felt skin and muscle tear, and a thick black fluid poured out of the wound onto his arms.

The u!xani roared and spun away from the sudden pain, dragging Zeke with her: He lost his grip on the weapon, and fell backward to the floor.

He saw Marty struggling to his feet.

"Fool," !Jng!xl said, rising. "Can you not kill two defenseless humans?"

!Dana reached down with a first-segment hand and ripped the !kan out of her belly, tossing it behind her. She roared again, in anger and pain, and began advancing on Zeke.

Marty shook his head, as if he were trying to clear it. Then he bent over and picked up one of the huge stone sculptures that dotted the office.

Holding it like a battering ram, he charged without warning.

The sculpture slammed into !Dana from behind. Caught off balance, she smashed hard, head first, into the window, with a loud, cracking noise.

!Jng!xl started toward them.

Zeke lunged across the floor and, in one fluid motion, picked up the !kan from where !Dana had tossed it and threw it at the Councilor. It caught !Jng!xl just beneath the hooded carapace that shielded her eyes.

She screamed in agony, and collapsed in a heap where she stood.

Behind him, by the window, Marty and !Dana both rose unsteadily. Marty got to his feet first, and rammed her again with the stone sculpture.

She slammed into the window. There was a large *crack*—and suddenly the window was gone.

Alarms began sounding, as a harsh arctic breeze whipped through the room.

!Dana teetered for a moment on the edge of the window. Then she fell through, and disappeared from sight.

"Damn worm," Marty said, dropping the statue.

The door to the Councilor's office dilated—and two u!xani charged into the room, followed by the male o!xer who had conducted the negotiations for kadak!xa.

"Councilor?" he began. "What is—"

Then he caught sight of Vajix!krk's body, sprawled across the table. His mandibles began clacking together in agitation.

"Who is responsible for this?"

"There!" !Jng!xl said, rising and pointing to Zeke. She had removed the !kan from beneath her eye, but blood was still dripping from the wound. "The human attacked me, and murdered your Councilor—kill him!"

The warriors started forward.

"Wait," Zeke said, panting, trying to catch his breath. "*She* killed your Councilor, not me. And I can prove it."

"Indeed," the male said. "How?"

"I've got the evidence on my ship. There's going to be a disaster here, and she intended to use that to—"

With a sudden roar, !Jng!xl leapt for him.

The two u!xani stepped into her path, and using their spinnerets, easily secured her.

"It appears we owe you a debt of thanks, Ezekiel Bones," the male said, as the u!xani led !Jng!xl away.

"Can we save the congratulations for later?" Marty asked, stepping back from the window. "I'm freezing."

"Of course," the male said, bowing. "I must inform my superiors, and the Diet at large, of this terrible tragedy."

Marty looked up at Zeke.

"The Diet."

Zeke's eyes widened.

"The challenge."

They broke into a dead run, heading for the door.

This carpet was made of a very unusual fabric, Jackson decided.

Twice now, the u!xani had aimed a spray of acid at him. Each time, she had missed, and each time, the acid had splattered harmlessly on the carpet. And he knew that acid was not harmless.

The u!xani had also nearly trapped him within her webbing once, but he was alert to the range of her spinnerets now, and stayed well beyond it.

Though the challenge thus far had been uneventful, Jackson had been studying his opponent carefully.

The u!xani was not as fast as he was, nor were her reflexes as quick.

Those were the only advantages he had—plus that interesting fact about the carpet.

Now she moved closer to him, still holding her bladed second segment off the ground.

Every other time she had approached he had used his speed to circle away, never allowing her to come within range to use her webs, or acid, on him. Now though, he simply moved back, edging slowly toward one of the corners of the carpet.

Behind the u!xani, he saw G!daeer click her first-segment claws together. He knew she thought he had blundered fatally, maneuvered himself into a trap from which he could not escape.

He hoped the u!xani was thinking the same thing.

She was close enough to him now. He allowed a brief flash of fear to shine in his eyes.

And then he stumbled.

With a roar, the u!xani charged.

Jackson rolled backward and lifted the edge of the carpet. Holding it over his head, he ran straight at the u!xani.

An opening on the side of her body dilated, and a stream of acid shot out, splashing harmlessly against the carpet Jackson now held in front of him as a shield.

The u!xani ran right into the carpet, but Jackson had already let it go. And in the instant the carpet struck her, temporarily hiding him, he was behind her.

He jumped onto her massive back and ripped at the gill fringes on her first segment with all his might. They stretched in his hand, like rubber. He pulled again. A piece of one tore off, and blood gushed out of the wound it made.

The u!xani roared in agony.

Snarling, she tried to reach around her body for him, but her arms were too short. Jackson yanked at her gills again.

She tried to roll over onto her back and crush him.

But he had expected that. The second she started to turn beneath him, he rolled off her and tumbled away, out of range.

Or so he planned.

In actuality, the u!xani did not complete her roll. Somehow, she managed to right herself. As Jackson came to his feet, a strand of her webbing shot out and grabbed his ankle. Another streamed past and caught his arm.

Within seconds, he was helpless, bound too securely to even move. It was just like the first !dza—the one where he had been truly lucky, and an earthquake had freed him from his bonds. It was too much to expect something exactly like that to happen again.

Roaring again, in pain and anger, the u!xani moved toward him.

Jackson found himself praying for the earth to shake, or the roof to cave in, or. . . .

The door to the Great Hall dilated, and a very beat-up looking Zeke Bones strode through, Marty and one of the smallest !xaka's he had ever seen a step behind him.

"Stop the fight," Zeke commanded instantly.

Jackson let out a sigh of relief. Maybe there was something to those rumors of his divinity, after all.

Then he noticed the u!xani was still snarling in pain, still coming for him.

"Hey!" he yelled. "Didn't you hear him? Stop!"

A series of clicks sounded from behind him, from where G!daeer had been watching the fight. Undoubtedly, she was urging the u!xani to finish him off.

But Zeke had seen what was happening now. He strode across the Hall quickly, and stepped directly in front of the u!xani.

"Stop," he said. "The challenge is not to take place."

The u!xani hiss/click!ed in anger.

The male G!at o!xer came and stood by Zeke's side. He ordered the u!xani back as well.

Finally, she slumped, and turned away from Jackson.

The male turned, and bowed before the dais.

"A terrible tragedy has occurred, Councilors," he said, and began to tell them of what had happened in the G!at tower.

Zeke and Marty helped Jackson to his feet, and began the sticky process of extricating him from the !xaka!'s webbing.

"This stuff is like steel cable," Zeke said.

G!daeer approached them, hate flashing in her eyes. As she drew near, she lifted her first two segments off the floor, raising them so that her eyes were on a level with Jackson's as she spoke.

"I would have liked to fight you myself. Then the honor of the u!xani would not be in disgrace."

"So you say," Jackson answered.

"You would never have tricked me, Jackson Charles," G!daeer said. "You are not u!xani."

"Maybe not," Jackson said, and then he flashed the !xaka! a big smile. "But I am divinely lucky."

On the dais, the !xamini Councilor had risen. "Bring the slave Kadak!xa forward."

Two o!xer escorted Kadak!xa from the galleries where she had been seated. She took her place alongside the G!at o!xer.

The male spoke. "In the interests of preserving harmony between the G!at and the human clan represented by Ezekiel Bones, we hereby renounce our claim to this slave." The male turned to Kadak!xa. "You are now free. Henceforth, the G!at will have no claim to you."

Kadak!xa nodded slightly.

Marty clapped.

"It is customary for you to make a statement to the Diet at this time," the male G!at told her.

"A statement?" Kadak!xa hissed. "Here is my statement."

She spat in front of the huge dais where the Councilors sat.

"May you all be consumed from within by parasites."

In the stunned silence that followed, she crossed the room and began to swiftly cut the webbing that bound Jackson.

Zeke detached himself from the group and approached the Diet.

"In recognition of the clan G!at's magnanimous gesture in freeing Kadak!xa," Zeke said. "I give them this." He handed the second folder to the male o!xer.

"Is this what the Councilor had agreed on?" the o!xer asked.

"It's what the Councilor deserved," Zeke replied. He turned to face the Diet.

"What I have just handed the o!xer," he said matter-of-factly, "is unequivocal proof that the clan G!at are not descendants of the original N'Gossans. That the G!at *!x'kuta* is a fiction. And that they have been aware of this for a century, and deliberately concealed the truth from the rest of you."

He nodded at the folder, which the o!xer had opened and was even now desperately scanning through.

"I promise you all copies within the hour."

He almost felt sorry for whoever the next G!at Councilor would be.

Almost.

"I should also tell you that during the course of my research, I came across another very interesting piece of information," Zeke said. "This whole island is sitting right next to a volcano—a very active volcano, on the verge of an explosion. All respect, Councilors—I suggest you evacuate immediately. I plan to do so."

He bowed slightly.

With that, the five of them—Zeke, Marty, Reelys, Jackson, and Kadak!xa—turned their backs on the

Supreme Council of the Diet of Monopolistics, and left the Great Hall for the last time.

The next day, the evacuation of N'Gossa began in earnest.

Two days later, the lower levels of the in!chi consular tower were finally reached. Shortly thereafter, a shuttle made its way from Ahng to the *Ostrom*.

"Hey, Zeke," Marty said, walking into the main lab. "Got a minute?"

"Hold on," Zeke said, not even looking up. He was hunched over the image of one of the N'Gossa A tablets. The fact that the inscriptions on these tablets were in a completely different language had sent him back to square one in the deciphering process—and two days later, that's where he still was. And the fact that the symbols were incidental to the ones used in N'Gossa B made it hard for him to attempt any translation without unconsciously using that language as a point of reference.

The simple fact that the G!at were not now, nor had they ever been, descendants of the original N'Gossa civilization, was all the information that the many clans who had been forced to acknowledge the G!at's preeminence for countless years had wanted or needed. The !van had already led a group of them in petitioning Reelys to reopen talks on the transfer station.

But it wasn't enough for Zeke. He had to know what the tablets said. What the true rulers of ancient N'Gossa had been like.

He took a quick sip of tea from his mug, and almost gagged. It had gotten ice cold.

That was strange. It seemed like only a minute ago it had been too hot to drink.

"Hey, Zeke!" Marty's voice rang out insistently. "I got something to show you."

"Mmmm," Zeke said. If he assigned each of the group-ings a certain numeric value, it might make it easier to spot any patterns in the tablets themselves. . . .

"Hey, don't you ever take a break?"

That wasn't Marty's voice.

He looked up.

Sylvie Pharr was standing over him, smiling, hands on her hips.

Alive.

He shook his head slowly back and forth.

"How—"

"Come on," she said, taking his hand. He rose from the desk slowly, still unable to believe his eyes. "All work and no play makes Zeke a dull boy."

Epilogue

Five days later, the *Ostrom* was still orbiting Ahng.

N'Gossa had been completely evacuated, and G!at scientists were even now studying ways to allow the volcano to vent its energy in smaller, less destructive explosions.

And Zeke was still trying to decipher the N'Gossa A inscriptions.

They were all in the main lab having breakfast around one of the large tables there: Zeke, Marty, Jackson, Reelys, Sylvie, and Kadak!xa. Most of the lab was covered with images of the tablets and page after page of hastily scribbled notes. Zeke had gone back to one of his previously attempted solutions, the one that had seemed to hold out the most hope for success. Earlier, he'd noted that an extremely large number of lines in each of the N'Gossa A tablets began with the same set of hieroglyphs. If he could figure out what that initial group of glyphs meant, it would be like being handed one of the corner pieces to a jigsaw puzzle—everything else would flow from it.

"But what kind of word starts off a sentence the same way every time?" he wondered aloud.

"An area code?" Marty suggested, reaching for a dish across the table.

"A curse," Kadak!xa offered.

"Names," Sylvie suggested. "Why couldn't they be names?"

"Starting off every sentence?" Zeke shook his head. "I don't know anyone who talks that way."

"I do," Sylvie said, sipping from her cup of coffee. "You do too," she said, speaking to Kadak!xa. "That's how your brother spoke."

Kadak!xa set down the bowl she had been eating from. "I believe you are right, Sylvie. Ho!xa was of course speaking universal pidgin to you—but even in our own language, one always begins a statement by addressing the one being spoken to by name."

Marty scowled at both of them. "You're not suggesting that the taga!xi are the descendants of the N'Gossa. . . ."

Sylvie shrugged. "You're the expert, Zeke. What do you think?"

"If she is right—" Marty began.

"She's right," Zeke said, remembering the taga!xi he'd seen in Sylvie's article. The ring of muscle between their middle two segments would give them more control over their bodies, make them more flexible so they could squeeze in and around the various rooms of the N'Gossa cave dwellings.

"She's right," he repeated, the certainty growing inside him.

"Wow," Jackson said. "Do you realize what this is going to do to the caste structure on Ahng?"

Zeke nodded. "I imagine it'll shake things up a bit."

"A bit? Doc," Jackson shook his head. "I don't think the volcano will end up doing as much damage."

Whether or not the taga!xi were descended from the original N'Gossans was a question it would take years to settle. But it took less than a day for Zeke to confirm that

Sylvie's guess about the initial hieroglyphs had been correct. They were names—and with that, he was off and
running in his translation.

Two days later, they left Ahng.

Zeke's last act was presenting a preliminary translation
of one of the N'Gossa A tablets to the assembled Diet.
The G!at *!x'kuta*, in fact. Which turned out to be not a
proclamation on the "principles of order," but a dialogue
between two !xaka! on the merits of differing social
structures.

He especially liked the part when the two N'Gossans,
in passing, condemned the fixed caste system for its
inefficiency—and slavery for its absolute immorality.

He made sure to point out those two sections.

At the Nemesis transfer point, they said their farewells.
Reelys was leaving aboard the *Keshir* for Griynsh. The
exposure of the G!at's deception, and the other clans'
desire for further talks on the transfer station had given the
shri an opportunity they now intended to make the most
of. The next round of talks would take place on Griynsh,
where they hoped to set an example for the !xaka!.

"Farewell, Ezekiel Bones," Reelys said, his'er image
speaking from the large viewscreen in the main lab.
"I hope we will see each other again soon."

Zeke hoped so too, though Reelys was old by shri stan-
dards, had been old when they'd first met in the Legion.
Still, s/he certainly got around. Maybe they would meet
again.

"Goodbye, Reelys—I can't thank you enough for your
help."

Kadak!xa shouldered her way into range of the
scanner.

"I would give you my thanks too, Reelys. Zeke tells me without your help, none of this would have happened."

"I think you would have eventually escaped without the help of any of us, Kadak!xa," Reelys said. "But I was glad to be of service. Farewell."

They watched the *Keshir* unhook from the transfer station, and begin a slow, majestic glide toward the distant stars.

Zeke sighed, and turned away from the comscreen. "Back to work."

Sylvie stood beside him. "What's the rush, Zeke?"

"Would you believe I have to get ready for class?" Zeke asked. "They've had holograms teaching them for a month now."

"I'm rather fond of holograms," Sylvie said.

"Besides," he said, a little more seriously, "don't you have another assignment to get to?"

"Next assignment?" Sylvie asked. "I've still got to finish writing this one! Besides, I need a break after all that excitement." She looked up at him. "I thought I might spend some time in New Haven City."

Zeke smiled. "All the more reason to get there quickly, then," he said. "Herb, take us home. Maximum acceleration."

"Herb?" Sylvie asked. "Who's Herb?"

The comscreen filled with his image.

"I'm Herb. You must be Sylvie Pharr. I'm delighted to finally meet you."

Sylvie laughed. "And I'm delighted to meet you, too." She turned to Zeke. "You know he looks awfully familiar . . ." She snapped her fingers.

"I got it. Oh, Zeke," she said, smiling. "That's great." She frowned suddenly. "Were you the one who cleaned up my cabin?"

"Guilty," Herb said. "But Zeke told me to."

Zeke shrugged. "We thought you were dead."

"Well. . . ." Sylvie said. "The least you can do is help me put it back the way it was. Come on, Zeke."

They set off down the corridor together.

"Hey, wait a minute," Marty called out after them. "Who is he? Who's Herb?"

Zeke turned back to him, shaking his head.

"Don't you want to earn that pizza?"

Sylvie stopped suddenly. "Pizza? What about pizza?"

"Zeke promised me three pies if I figured out who Herb was," Marty said. He lowered his voice. "I'll cut you in on it if you give me a clue."

"Hey, that's not fair!" Zeke said.

"What about it, Sylvie?"

"I'm thinking." She peered at Marty and raised an eyebrow. "How much of that pizza do I get?"

Marty exhaled in disgust. "Forget it," he said. "I'll figure it out myself."

"Suit yourself," Sylvie said—and then burst out laughing. She and Zeke disappeared down the corridor.

Marty turned back to the comscreen.

The image of H.G. (Herbert George) Wells peered back at him impassively.

The *Ostrom* streaked through the stars, heading for Earth.

Appendix

Notes on !Xaka! Society

THE MAJOR CLAN GROUPS:

G*!at* (*guh-at*)—The oldest and most powerful of all the clans. Claiming descent from the high priests of ancient N'Gossa, they have dominated Ahng's affairs through tight control of the planet's natural resources. As the !xaka! empire spread across neighboring sectors of the galaxy, their control has been somewhat loosened.

!van (*sh-van*)—Actually a conglomerate of many smaller, older clans. Their meteoric rise in !xaka! affairs over the last fifty years is due largely to their successful importation and imitation of much human computer technology.

Ghi!reeli (*gi-uh-real-ee*)—By the mid-twenty-fifth century, notable mainly for their total subservience to G!at interests. They control many transportation interests on Ahng.

in!chi (*in-uh-kiy*)—Somewhat of an anomaly, in that this clan was formed in fairly recent times by a consortium of wealthy o!xer in order to assert their power more successfully.

!xamini (*ʒha-mean-ee*)—Once one of the more power-ful clans, their influence has waned as the fossil fuel reserves they controlled became depleted.

THE CASTE STRUCTURE:

Beyond the four very broad categories of slave, soldier, worker and Councilor, the !xaka! caste system cannot easily be translated into human equivalents. Though the hierarchy generally follows the above structure, many exceptions exist. Scientists, for example, attach them-selves to particular Councilor/sponsors, and their status rises and falls as does that of their sponsor. Two frequently used terms are also worth defining:

o!xer (*o-share*)—a generic name for mid-level bureau-crats of all clans.

u!xani (*oo-shan-ee*)—Literally, "those of the u!xan." In ancient times a warrior cult, the u!xani today are an elite fighting corps who consider themselves outside the for-mal caste structure. Though historically associated with the G!at, the u!xani in fact have no particular clan affil-iation and form special divisions within all the clan armies.

Technical Data Bank

Getting to examine the N'Gossa Scrolls, one of the great archeological treasures of the galaxy, was an unexpected bonus for Ezekiel Bones.

His trip to Ahng, the home world of the !xaka!, was a desperate mission to rescue his friend and shipmate, Kadakalxa, from slavery. In order to do that, he needed to decipher the N'Gossa scrolls.

More critical, perhaps, was Zeke's discovery—with the aid of Marty Szigmond—that N'Gossa Island sat atop an ancient, active volcano that was due for a major eruption. It was during their underwater investigation of the sunken ruins of N'Gossa that Marty was able to find the evidence to convince the G!at and the other clans that they were in immediate danger.

Linguistics is not Dr. Bones's specialty, but his perseverance, ingenious deductions, and a helpful computer led him to a surprising translation of the texts. The ruling G!at clan's claims of priestly descent and superiority were challenged by Bones's work, as was their official translation of the N'Gossa scrolls.

Yet Bones's greatest discovery, based on his new translation of the scrolls, caused a more profound

shake-up in !xakan! society than any volcanic eruption. His conclusion that the low-ranking Taga!xi clan
were the true descendents of the ancient N'Gossans,
and not the G!at, was the basis of a political and social
revolution.

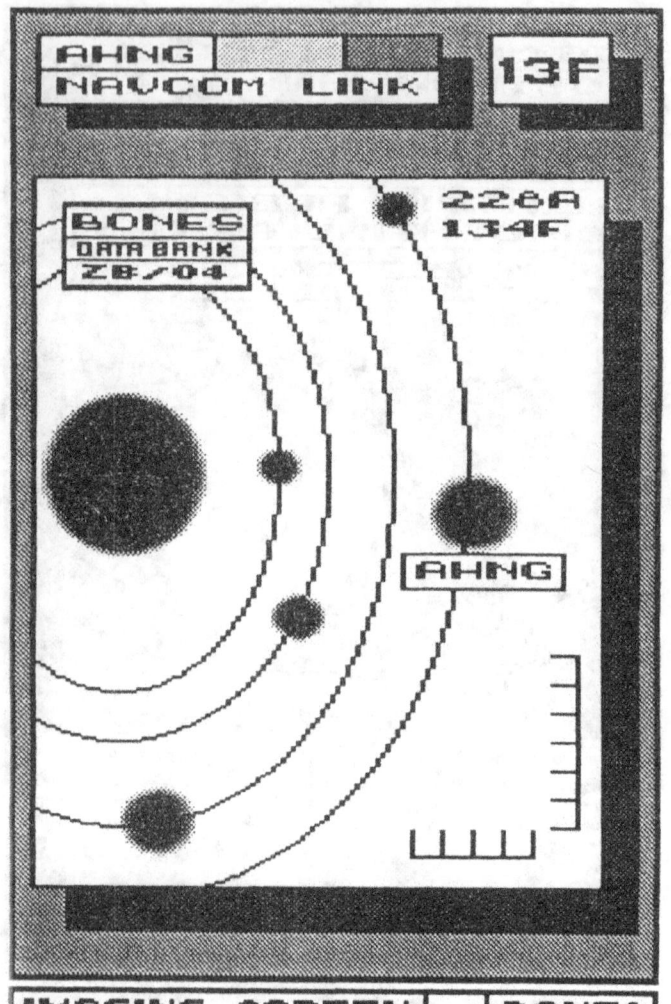

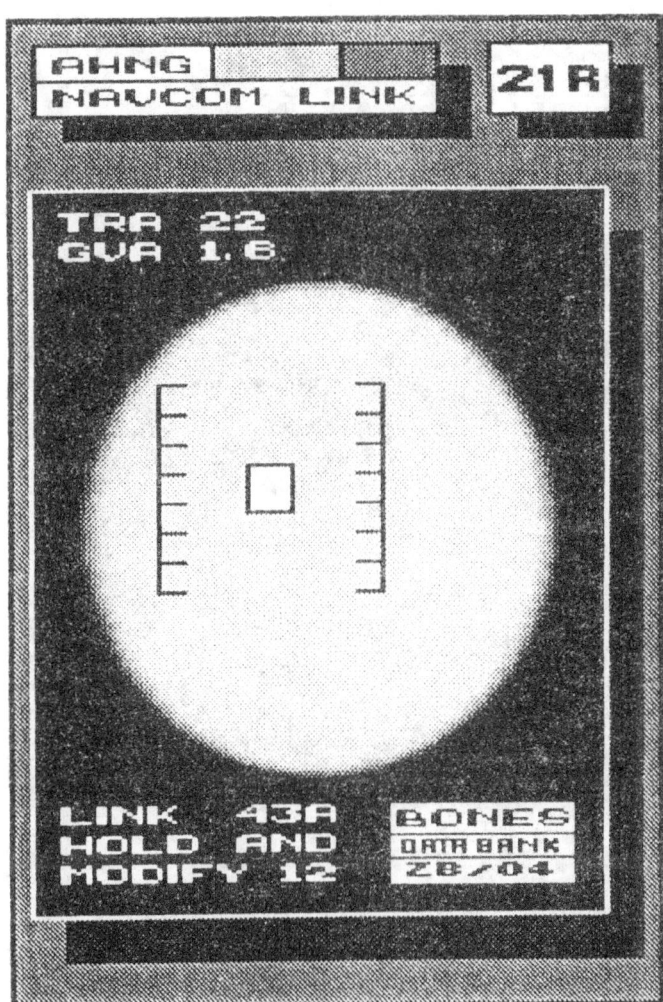

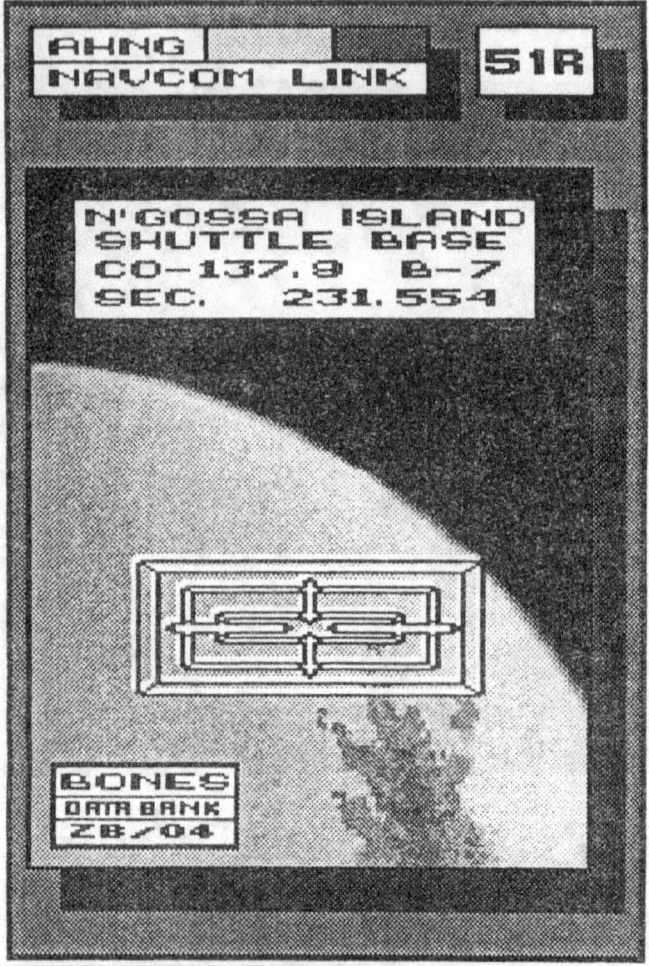

AHNG
NAVCOM LINK
51R

N'GOSSA ISLAND
SHUTTLE BASE
CO-137.9 B-7
SEC.   231.554

BONES
DATA BANK
ZB/04

IMAGING SCREEN   BONES
N'GOSSA ISLAND

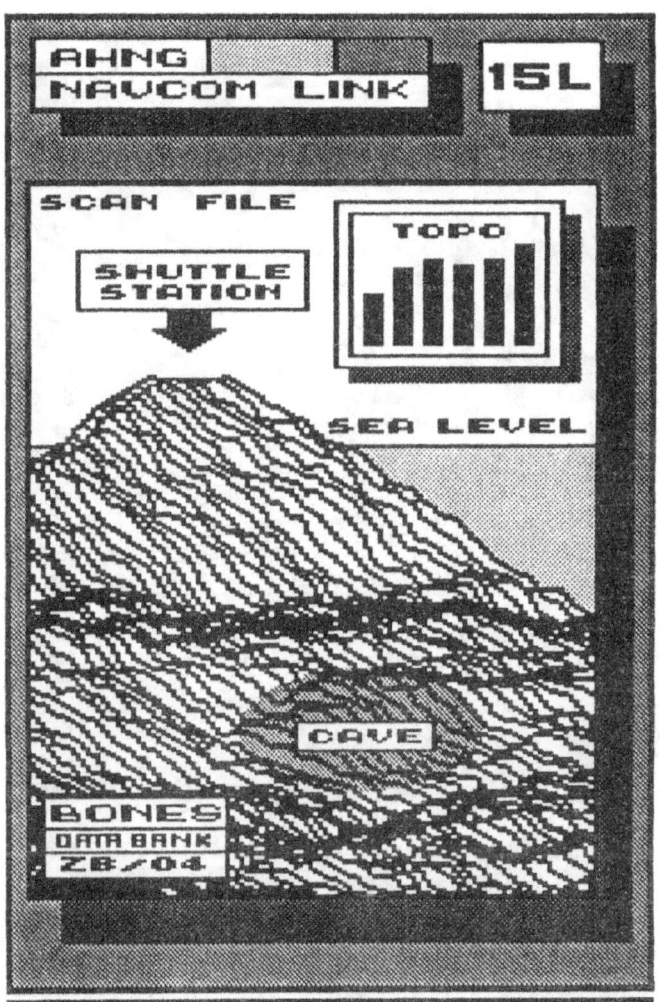

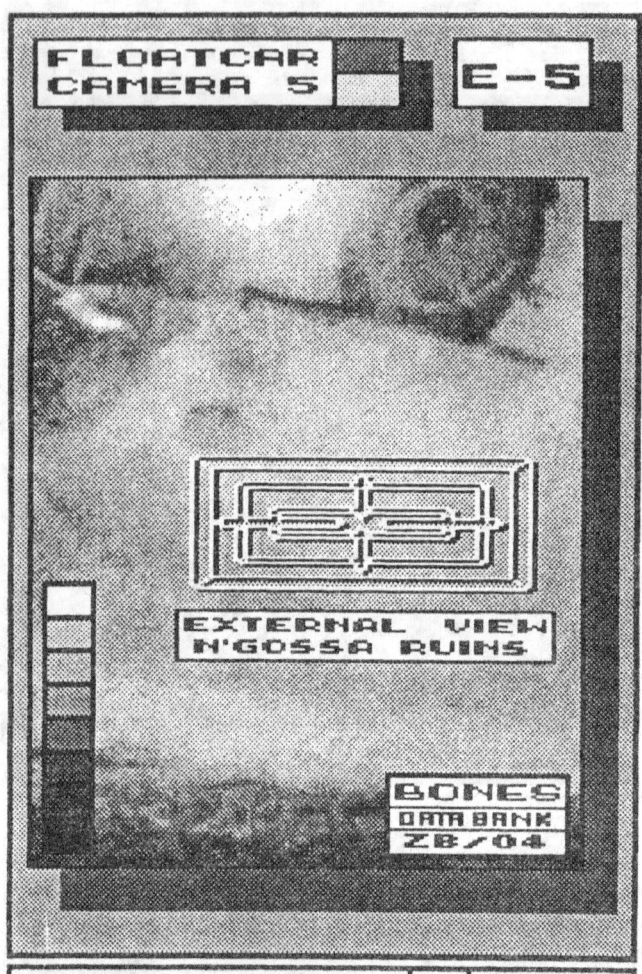

FLOATCAR
CAMERA 5

E-5

EXTERNAL VIEW
N'GOSSA RUINS

BONES
DATA BANK
ZB/04

IMAGING SCREEN | BONES
UNDERWATER IMAGING

FLOATCAR
CAMERA 5

E-5

BONES
DATA BANK
ZB/04

IMAGING SCREEN | BONES
PILLOW LAVA

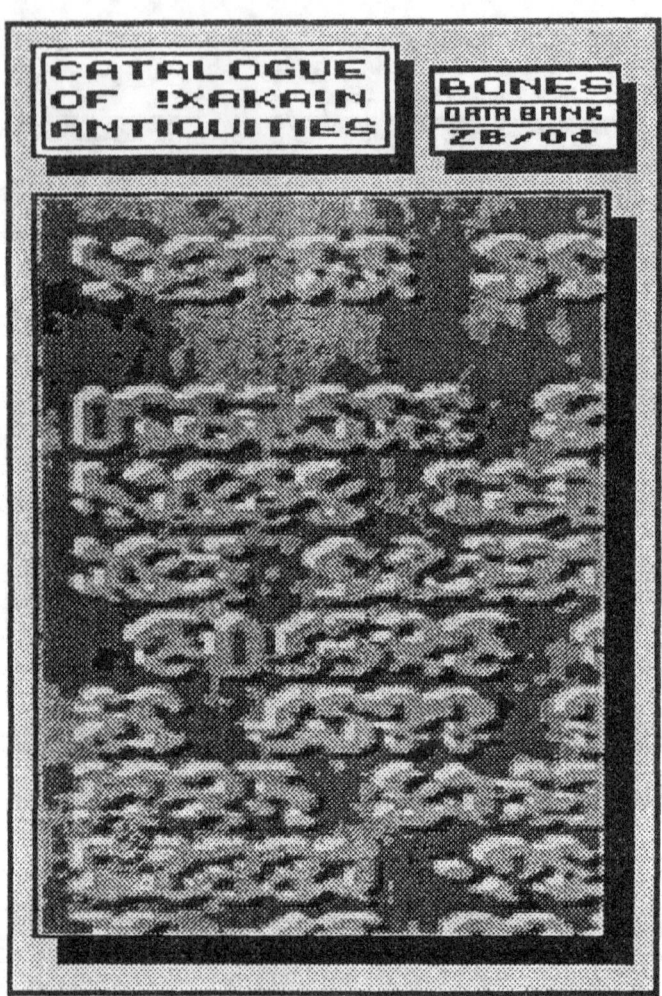

CATALOGUE OF !XAKA!N ANTIQUITIES

BONES DATA BANK ZB/04

IMAGING SCREEN | **BONES**

IMAGE PROCESSING

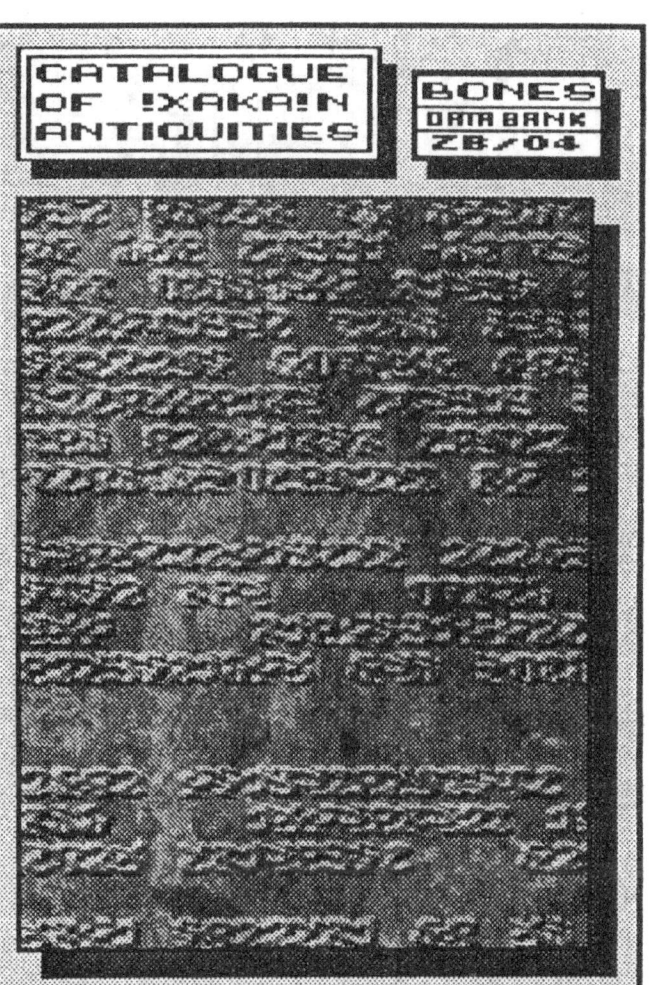

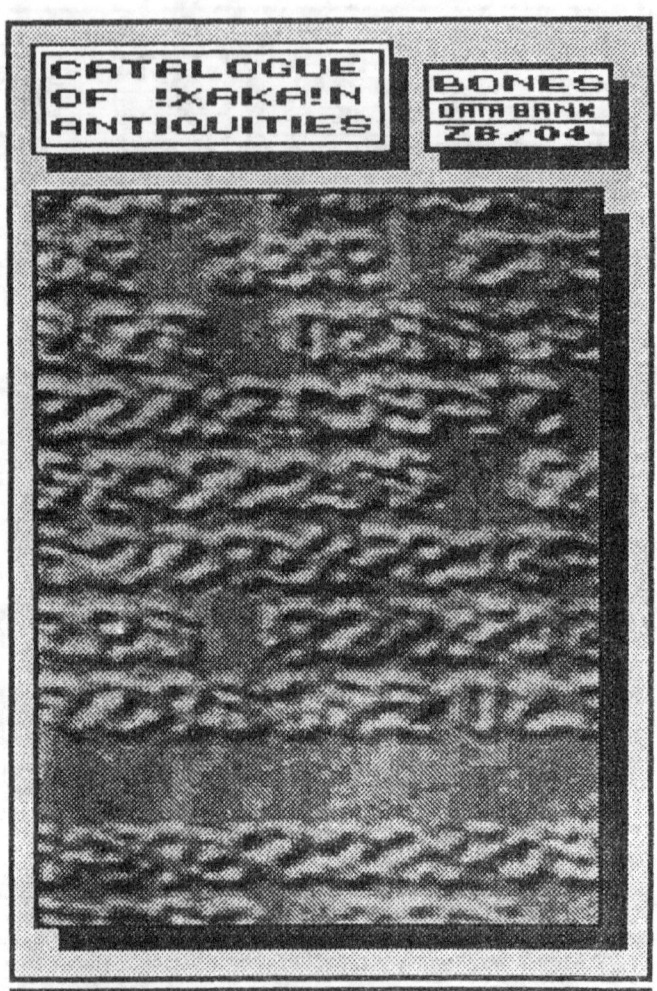

CATALOGUE OF !XAKA!N ANTIQUITIES

BONES DATA BANK ZB/04

IMAGING SCREEN | **BONES**

N'GOSSA "B" SCROLL

CATALOGUE OF !XAKA!N ANTIQUITIES

BONES DATA BANK ZB/04

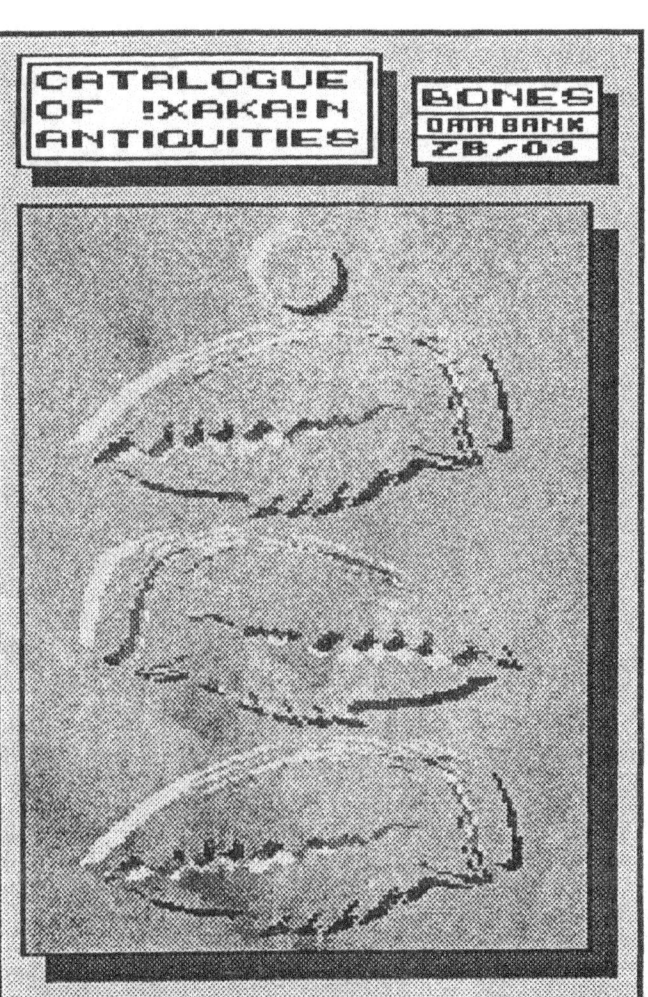

IMAGING SCREEN | **BONES**
!XAMINI CLAN BADGE

CATALOGUE OF !XAKA!N ANTIQUITIES

BONES DATA BANK ZB/04

IMAGING SCREEN | BONES
!VAN CLAN BADGE